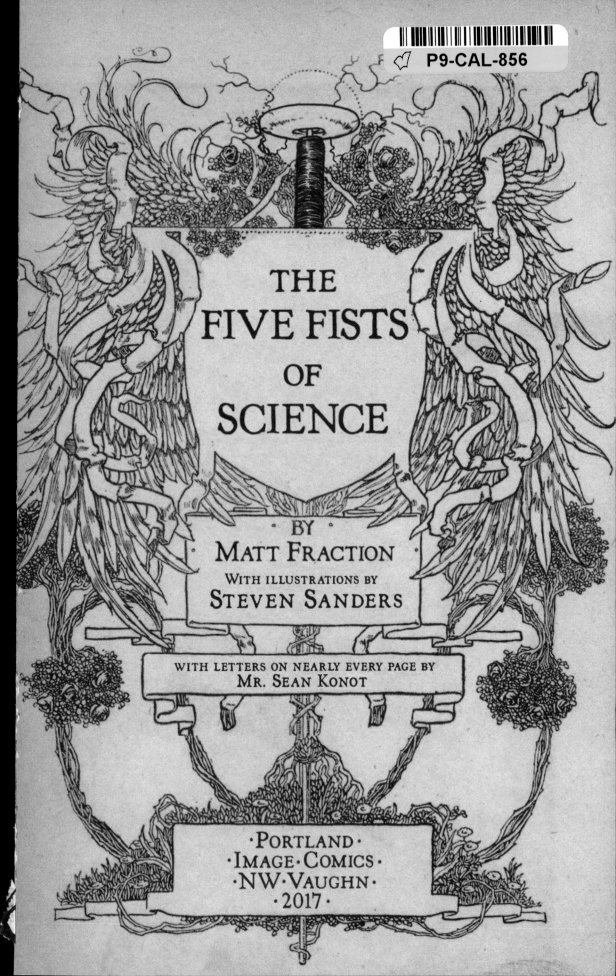

THE
FIVE FISTS
OF
SCIENCE

· BY ·
MATT FRACTION

WITH ILLUSTRATIONS BY
STEVEN SANDERS

WITH LETTERS ON NEARLY EVERY PAGE BY
MR. SEAN KONOT

· PORTLAND ·
· IMAGE · COMICS ·
· NW · VAUGHN ·
· 2017 ·

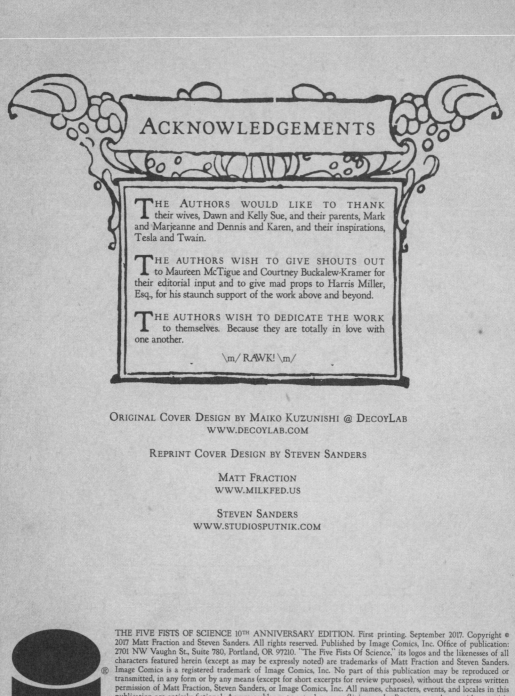

Acknowledgements

The Authors would like to thank their wives, Dawn and Kelly Sue, and their parents, Mark and Marjeanne and Dennis and Karen, and their inspirations, Tesla and Twain.

The authors wish to give shouts out to Maureen McTigue and Courtney Buckalew-Kramer for their editorial input and to give mad props to Harris Miller, Esq., for his staunch support of the work above and beyond.

The authors wish to dedicate the work to themselves. Because they are totally in love with one another.

\m/ RAWK! \m/

Original Cover Design by Maiko Kuzunishi @ DecoyLab
WWW.DECOYLAB.COM

Reprint Cover Design by Steven Sanders

Matt Fraction
WWW.MILKFED.US

Steven Sanders
WWW.STUDIOSPUTNIK.COM

THE FIVE FISTS OF SCIENCE 10TH ANNIVERSARY EDITION. First printing. September 2017.

Published by Image Comics, Inc. Office of publication: 2701 NW Vaughn St., Suite 780, Portland, OR 97210.

Printed in the U.S.A. For information regarding the CPSIA on this printed material call: 203-595-3636 and provide reference # RICH – 761219. ISBN: 978-1-5343-0436-9

Matt Fraction & Steven Sanders representation: Shep Rosenman & Caitlin DiMotta of KGR, LLP in Santa Monica, CA.

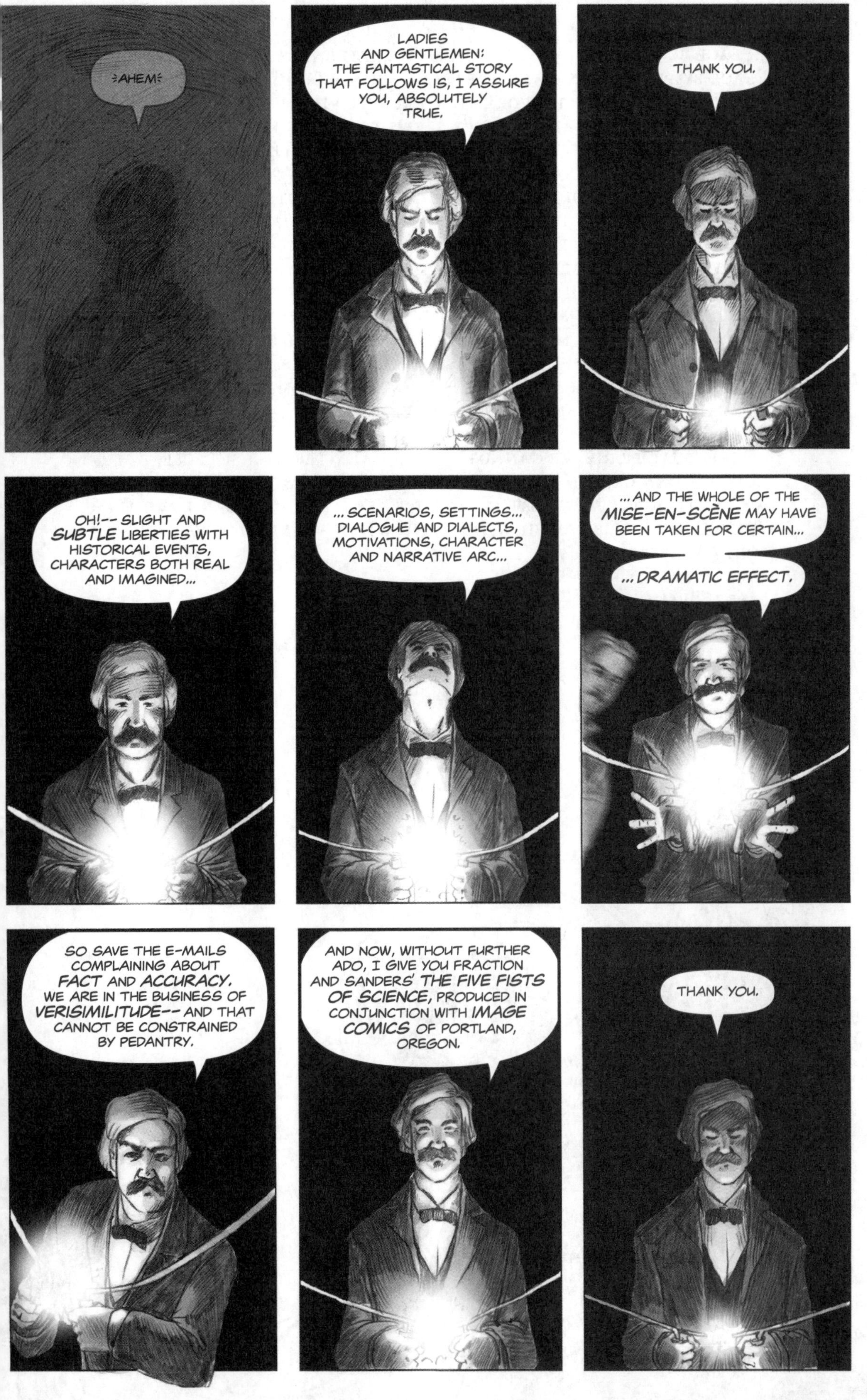
AHEM
LADIES AND GENTLEMEN: THE FANTASTICAL STORY THAT FOLLOWS IS, I ASSURE YOU, ABSOLUTELY TRUE.
THANK YOU.
OH!-- SLIGHT AND SUBTLE LIBERTIES WITH HISTORICAL EVENTS, CHARACTERS BOTH REAL AND IMAGINED...
...SCENARIOS, SETTINGS... DIALOGUE AND DIALECTS, MOTIVATIONS, CHARACTER AND NARRATIVE ARC...
...AND THE WHOLE OF THE MISE-EN-SCÈNE MAY HAVE BEEN TAKEN FOR CERTAIN...
...DRAMATIC EFFECT.
SO SAVE THE E-MAILS COMPLAINING ABOUT FACT AND ACCURACY. WE ARE IN THE BUSINESS OF VERISIMILITUDE-- AND THAT CANNOT BE CONSTRAINED BY PEDANTRY.
AND NOW, WITHOUT FURTHER ADO, I GIVE YOU FRACTION AND SANDERS' THE FIVE FISTS OF SCIENCE, PRODUCED IN CONJUNCTION WITH IMAGE COMICS OF PORTLAND, OREGON.
THANK YOU.

...PEACE BY COMPULSION. THAT SEEMS A BETTER IDEA THAN THE OTHER. PEACE BY PERSUASION HAS A PLEASANT SOUND, BUT I THINK WE SHOULD NOT BE ABLE TO WORK IT. WE SHOULD HAVE TO TAME THE HUMAN RACE FIRST, AND HISTORY SEEMS TO SHOW THAT THAT CANNOT BE DONE. CAN'T WE REDUCE THE ARMAMENTS LITTLE BY LITTLE - ON A PRO RATA BASIS - BY CONCERT OF THE POWERS? CAN'T WE GET FOUR GREAT POWERS TO AGREE TO REDUCE THEIR STRENGTH 10 PERCENT A YEAR AND THRASH THE OTHERS INTO DOING LIKEWISE? FOR, OF COURSE, WE CANNOT EXPECT ALL OF THE POWERS TO BE IN THEIR RIGHT MINDS AT ONE TIME. IT HAS BEEN TRIED. WE ARE NOT GOING TO TRY TO GET ALL OF THEM TO GO INTO THE SCHEME PEACEABLY, ARE WE? IN THAT CASE I MUST WITHDRAW MY INFLUENCE; BECAUSE, FOR BUSINESS REASONS, I MUST PRESERVE THE OUTWARD SIGNS OF SANITY. FOUR IS ENOUGH IF THEY CAN BE SECURELY HARNESSED TOGETHER. THEY CAN COMPEL PEACE, AND PEACE WITHOUT COMPULSION WOULD BE AGAINST NATURE AND NOT OPERATIVE.

...PERPETUAL PEACE WE CANNOT HAVE ON ANY TERMS, I SUPPOSE; BUT I HOPE WE CAN GRADUALLY REDUCE THE WAR STRENGTH OF EUROPE TILL WE GET IT DOWN TO WHERE IT OUGHT TO BE... THEN WE CAN HAVE ALL THE PEACE THAT IS WORTH WHILE, AND WHEN WE WANT A WAR ANY-BODY CAN AFFORD IT.

MARK TWAIN
JANUARY 9, 1899

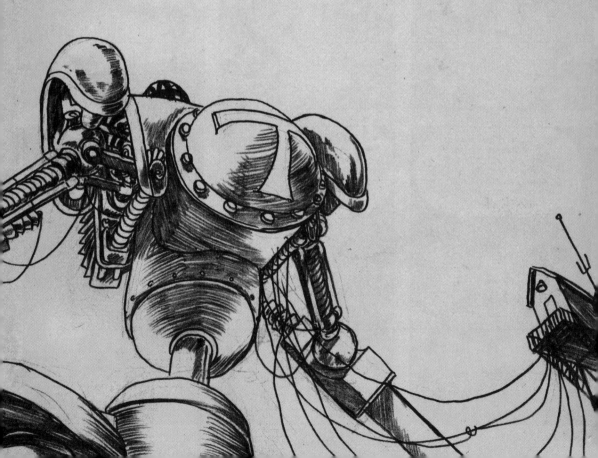

...(T)HE ART I HAVE EVOLVED DOES NOT CONTEMPLATE MERELY THE CHANGE OF DIRECTION OF A MOVING VESSEL; IT AFFORDS MEANS OF ABSOLUTELY CONTROLLING, IN EVERY RESPECT, ALL THE INNUMERABLE TRANSLATORY (SIC) MOVEMENTS, AS WELL AS THE OPERATIONS OF ALL THE INTERNAL ORGANS, NO MATTER HOW MANY, OF AN INDIVIDUALIZED AUTOMATON. CRITICISMS TO THE EFFECT THAT THE CONTROL OF THE AUTOMATON COULD BE INTER-FERED WITH WERE MADE BY PEOPLE WHO DO NOT EVEN DREAM OF THE WONDERFUL RESULTS WHICH CAN BE ACCOMPLISHED BY USE OF ELECTRICAL VIBRATIONS. THE WORLD MOVES SLOWLY, AND NEW TRUTHS ARE DIFFICULT TO SEE. CERTAINLY, BY THE USE OF THIS PRINCIPLE, AN ARM FOR ATTACK AS WELL AS DEFENSE MAY BE PRO-VIDED, OF A DESTRUCTIVENESS ALL THE GREATER AS THE PRIN-CIPLE IS APPLICABLE TO SUBMARINE AND AERIAL VESSELS. THERE IS VIRTUALLY NO RESTRICTION AS TO THE AMOUNT OF EXPLOSIVE IT CAN CARRY, OR AS TO THE DISTANCE AT WHICH IT CAN STRIKE, AND FAILURE IS ALMOST IMPOSSIBLE. BUT THE FORCE OF THIS NEW PRINCIPLE DOES NOT WHOLLY RESIDE IN ITS DESTRUCTIVE-NESS. ITS ADVENT INTRODUCES INTO WARFARE AN ELEMENT WHICH NEVER EXISTED BEFORE—A FIGHTING-MACHINE WITHOUT MEN AS A MEANS OF ATTACK AND DEFENSE. THE CONTINUOUS DE-VELOPMENT IN THIS DIRECTION MUST ULTIMATELY MAKE WAR A MERE CONTEST OF MACHINES WITHOUT MEN AND WITHOUT LOSS OF LIFE-- A CONDITION WHICH WOULD HAVE BEEN IMPOSSIBLE WITHOUT THIS NEW DEPARTURE, AND WHICH, IN MY OPINION, MUST BE REACHED AS PRELIMINARY TO PERMANENT PEACE. THE FUTURE WILL EITHER BEAR OUT OR DISPROVE THESE VIEWS. MY IDEAS ON THIS SUBJECT HAVE BEEN PUT FORTH WITH DEEP CON-VICTION, BUT IN A HUMBLE SPIRIT.

THE ESTABLISHMENT OF PERMANENT PEACEFUL RELATIONS BE-TWEEN NATIONS WOULD MOST EFFECTIVELY REDUCE THE FORCE RETARDING THE HUMAN MASS, AND WOULD BE THE BEST SOLU-TION OF THIS GREAT HUMAN PROBLEM. BUT WILL THE DREAM OF UNIVERSAL PEACE EVER BE REALIZED? LET US HOPE THAT IT WILL. WHEN ALL DARKNESS SHALL BE DISSIPATED BY THE LIGHT OF SCI-ENCE, WHEN ALL NATIONS SHALL BE MERGED INTO ONE, AND PA-TRIOTISM SHALL BE IDENTICAL WITH RELIGION, WHEN THERE SHALL BE ONE LANGUAGE, ONE COUNTRY, ONE END, THEN THE DREAM WILL HAVE BECOME REALITY.

FROM "THE PROBLEM OF INCREASING HUMAN ENERGY," BY NIKOLA TESLA

CENTURY ILLUSTRATED MAGAZINE, JANUARY, 1900.

OUR CHARACTERS

MARK TWAIN (1835 - 1910): BORN DURING THE APPEARANCE OF HALLEY'S COMET AS SAMUEL LANGHORNE CLEMENS IN FLORIDA, MISSOURI, TWAIN WENT WEST TIN-PANNING FOR GOLD AND EVENTUALLY ENDED UP A WRITER IN SAN FRANCISCO. HE WROTE THE INNOCENTS ABROAD, THE ADVENTURES OF TOM SAWYER, AND THE BOOK HEMINGWAY SAID ALL AMERICAN LITERATURE CAME FROM, THE ADVENTURES OF HUCKLEBERRY FINN. TRULY THE FIRST AMERICAN CELEBRITY, TWAIN WINED AND DINED WITH EVERYONE WHO WAS ANYONE-- AND COUNTED AMONGST HIS FANS THE BRILLIANT YOUNG INVENTOR NIKOLA TESLA. BANKRUPTED BY DODGY INVESTMENTS, PLAGUED BY BAD BUSINESS DECISIONS, AND MOURNING THE DEATH OF HIS DAUGHTER, TWAIN AND HIS FAMILY LEFT FOR EUROPE IN 1898 UNDER "FINANCIAL EXILE." HE BECAME INVOLVED WITH THE ARMISTICE MOVEMENT WHILE IN VIENNA, WHERE HE WAS KNOWN AS "OUR FAMOUS GUEST."

NIKOLA TESLA (1856 - 1943): A SERBIAN SCIENTIST AND INVENTOR, TESLA INVENTED ALTERNATING CURRENT, THE SPARK PLUG, AND THE FIRST RADIO TRANSMITTER-- A FEAT THAT WOULD ONLY BE RECOGNIZED POSTHUMOUSLY BY THE SUPREME COURT. DEATHLY ILL IN HIS YOUTH, TESLA CLAIMED IT WAS READING THE WORKS OF MARK TWAIN (AND LAUGHING) THAT SAVED HIS LIFE. THOMAS EDISON HIRED TESLA AND LATER DEFRAUDED HIM-- SETTING THE STAGE FOR PERSONAL ANIMOSITY AND A "WAR OF THE CURRENTS" BETWEEN TESLA'S ALTERNATING CURRENT AND EDISON'S DIRECT CURRENT. TESLA'S FORTUNES ROSE AND FELL WILDLY THROUGHOUT HIS LIFE, BUT IN 1899, HE WAS LIVING IN NEW YORK CITY, WORKING IN HIS LAB AT 46-48 HOUSTON STREET, AND WAS THE TOAST OF MANHATTAN NIGHTLIFE. WE HAVE MADE UP NONE OF THE MAN'S PERSONAL QUIRKS, PHOBIAS, OR FOIBLES, EXCEPT FOR THE DRESSING UP AND FIGHTING CRIME BIT.

BERTHA SOPHIE FELICITAS FREIFRAU VON SUTTNER (BARONESS BERTHA VON SUTTNER) (1843 - 1914): AN AUSTRIAN WRITER DEEPLY INVOLVED IN THE ARMISTICE MOVEMENT STARTING WITH THE PUBLICATION OF HER NOVEL LAY DOWN YOUR ARMS! IN 1889. THAT SHE WAS ALFRED NOBEL'S HOUSEKEEPER AND SECRETARY ALLOWED HER A LONG CORRESPONDENCE WITH NOBEL; IT'S BELIEVED THAT THE NOTION OF A NOBEL "PEACE PRIZE" WAS, IN FACT, HERS-- AND SHE WON IT IN 1905. IN REAL LIFE, SHE WAS MARRIED, SECRETLY AT FIRST, TO AUTHOR AND ENGINEER BARON ARTHUR GUNDACCAR VON SUTTNER, BUT THIS IS A COMIC BOOK SO WE DON'T HAVE TO CONCERN OURSELVES WITH SUCH DETAILS. WE HAVE TAKEN GREAT LIBERTIES WITH THE BARONESS' AGE AND APPEARANCE WITHIN OUR PAGES AND FOR THIS WE SHOULD PROBABLY APOLOGIZE.

TIMOTHY BOONE (1884 - 1975): WHOLLY FICTIONAL. WHOOP-DEE-DO, WHOOP-DEE-DO.

OUR CHARACTERS

JOHN PIERPONT MORGAN (1837 - 1913): A BANKER AND FINANCIER THAT, IN 1895, FOUNDED J.P. MORGAN & CO. WITH ITS NUMEROUS INTERNATIONAL BANKING ASSOCIATIONS, J.P. MORGAN & CO. BECAME STUNNINGLY POWERFUL-- THEY FOUNDED THE FIRST BILLION DOLLAR COMPANY, U.S. STEEL, AND FLOATED A $62 MILLION DOLLAR LOAN TO THE U.S. TREASURY TO RAISE THE SURPLUS TO $100 MILLION. A NOTED ART, BOOK, AND ANTIQUITIES COLLECTOR, MUCH OF MORGAN'S COLLECTION TODAY POPULATES THE METROPOLITAN MUSEUM OF ART. THESE TWO FACTS-- THAT HE WAS RICHER THAN GOD, AND HE WAS INTO ART, BOOKS, AND ANTIQUITIES, ALLOWED US TO EXTRAPOLATE THE DEMENTED CHARACTER THAT APPEARS IN THESE PAGES. IN REAL LIFE, MORGAN WAS NOT A BLACK MAGICIAN-- HE WAS A PROTESTANT.

THOMAS ALVA EDISON (1847 - 1931): "THE WIZARD OF MENLO PARK" WAS A FAMED INVENTOR, INDUSTRIALIST, AND HOLDER OF 1,093 PATENTS. THOMAS EDISON STARTED THE EDISON ELECTRIC LIGHT COMPANY WITH FINANCING PROVIDED BY J.P. MORGAN IN 1879. BY 1882, HIS PEARL STREET STATION UTILITY PROVIDED ELECTRICITY TO THE 50-SOME CUSTOMERS LIVING AROUND THE STATION. HIS MORGAN-BACKED DIRECT CURRENT SYSTEM WAS UNSAFE COMPARED TO TESLA'S ALTERNATING CURRENT SYSTEM-- YOU'D NEVER KNOW IT, THOUGH, AS EDISON ENGAGED IN A DISINFORMATION CAMPAIGN AGAINST AC THAT SAW THE INVENTION OF THE ELECTRIC CHAIR AND THE ELECTROCUTION OF AN ELEPHANT NAMED "TOPSY" AMONGST OTHER THINGS. EDISON FINANCED GUGLIELMO MARCONI'S WORK DEVELOPING RADIO AND HOLDS THE PATENT FOR THE MOTION PICTURE CAMERA. THE STORY GOES THAT HOLLYWOOD WAS STARTED IN THE CALIFORNIA DESERT BECAUSE MOVIE PRODUCERS WANTED TO BE AS FAR AWAY FROM EDISON AS POSSIBLE.

GUGLIELMO MARCONI (1874 - 1937): AN ENGINEER OF ITALIAN DESCENT AND NOBEL PRIZE WINNER, MARCONI'S WIRELESS TELEGRAPHY SYSTEM-- THE RADIO-- WAS PRECEDED BY A SYSTEM FIRST THEORETICALLY DEMONSTRATED BY NIKOLA TESLA THREE YEARS PRIOR. THIS WAS EVENTUALLY RECOGNIZED BY THE SUPREME COURT IN 1943, EVEN THOUGH MARCONI IS STILL KNOWN AS "THE FATHER OF RADIO." LATER IN LIFE, HE AND TESLA MENDED FENCES, BUT STILL. MARCONI WAS A MEMBER OF THE FASCIST GRAND COUNCIL IN ITALY-- MUSSOLINI WAS THE BEST MAN AT HIS WEDDING, EVEN. WE KNOW OF NO EVIDENCE THAT PROVES HIM THE STRESS-EATER WE PRESENT IN THESE PAGES, BUT IT WAS FUNNIER THAN MAKING HIM A FASCIST.

ANDREW CARNEGIE (1835 - 1919): A SCOTTISH BUSINESSMAN, FINANCIER, AND STEEL MAGNATE, CARNEGIE IS PROBABLY BEST KNOWN AS A PHILANTHROPIST WHO GAVE AWAY ALMOST $400 MILLION DOLLARS BY THE TIME OF HIS DEATH. HE WAS THE AUTHOR OF THE GOSPEL OF WEALTH, IN WHICH HE ESPOUSED A PERSONAL PHILOSOPHY THAT THE WEALTHY SHOULD HELP UPLIFT THEIR FELLOW MAN. OUR RANCID CHARACTER ASSASSINATION OF THIS MAN (AT LEAST BY ASSOCIATION) IS PREDICATED SOLELY ON CARNEGIE SELLING HIS INTERESTS IN CARNEGIE STEEL TO J.P. MORGAN IN 1901, PAVING THE WAY FOR THE INCEPTION OF U.S. STEEL. REALLY, THOUGH, HE SEEMS TO HAVE BEEN QUITE THE NICE GUY.

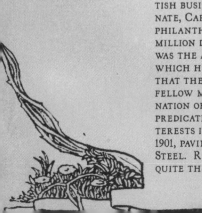

INQUIRIES

CONCERNING

THE

FIVE FISTS

OF

SCIENCE

EIGHTEENTH EDITION.

LONDON :

JOHN MURRAY, ALBEMARLE STREET.

1899.

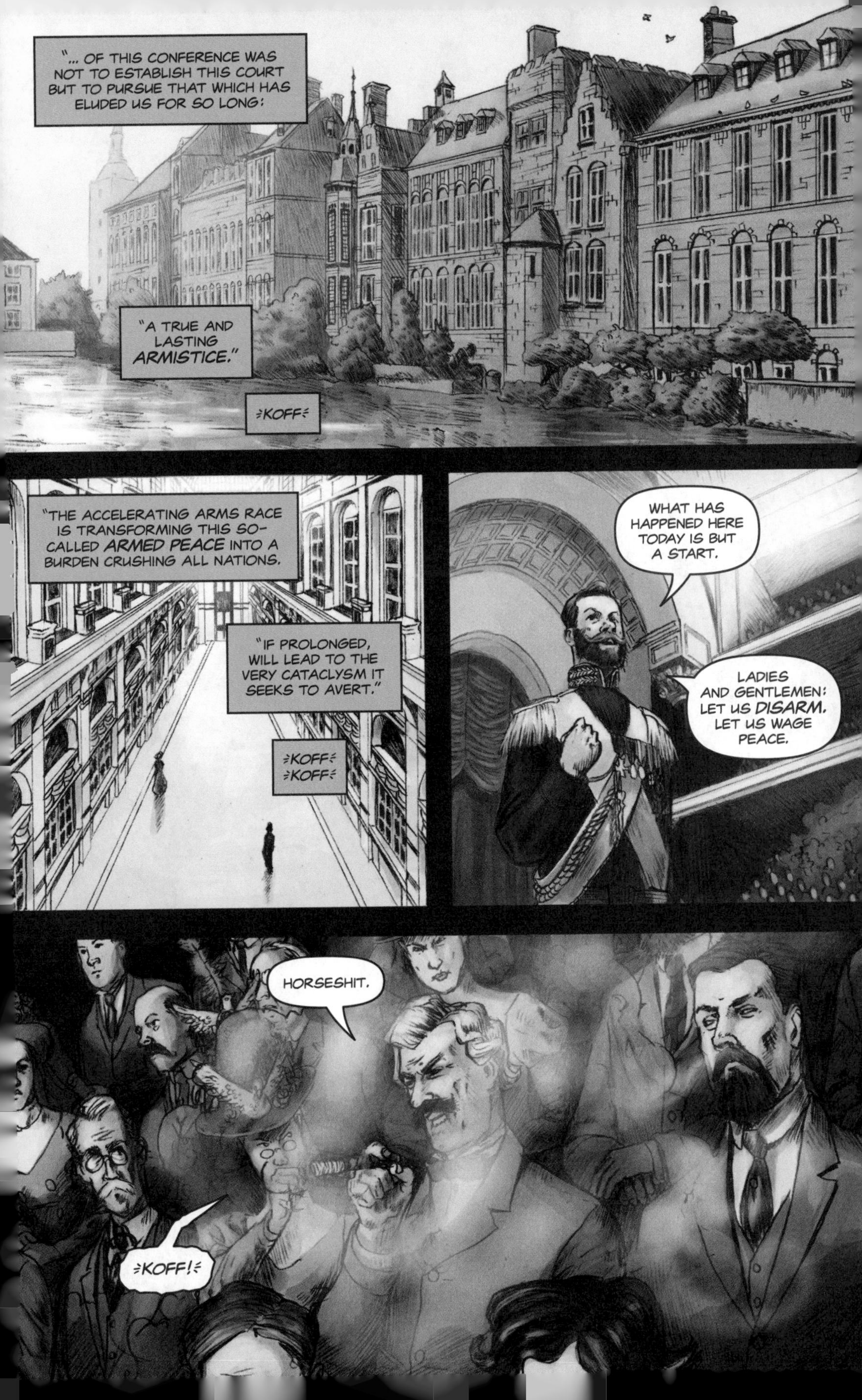
"... OF THIS CONFERENCE WAS NOT TO ESTABLISH THIS COURT BUT TO PURSUE THAT WHICH HAS ELUDED US FOR SO LONG:
"A TRUE AND LASTING ARMISTICE."
KOFF
"THE ACCELERATING ARMS RACE IS TRANSFORMING THIS SO-CALLED ARMED PEACE INTO A BURDEN CRUSHING ALL NATIONS.
"IF PROLONGED, WILL LEAD TO THE VERY CATACLYSM IT SEEKS TO AVERT."
KOFF KOFF
WHAT HAS HAPPENED HERE TODAY IS BUT A START.
LADIES AND GENTLEMEN: LET US DISARM. LET US WAGE PEACE.
HORSESHIT.
KOFF!

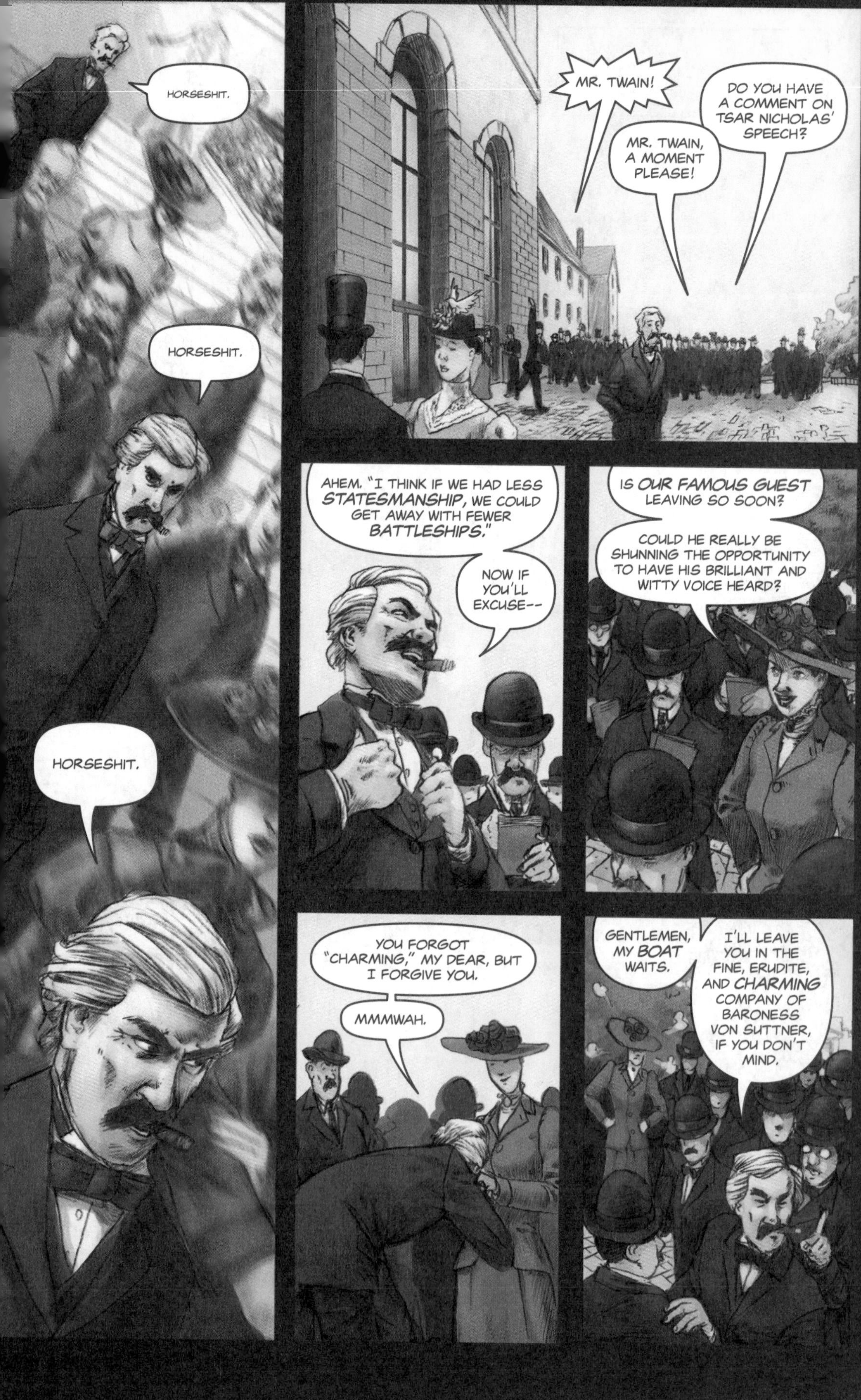
HORSESHIT.
HORSESHIT.
HORSESHIT.
MR. TWAIN!
MR. TWAIN, A MOMENT PLEASE!
DO YOU HAVE A COMMENT ON TSAR NICHOLAS' SPEECH?
AHEM. "I THINK IF WE HAD LESS STATESMANSHIP, WE COULD GET AWAY WITH FEWER BATTLESHIPS."
NOW IF YOU'LL EXCUSE--
IS OUR FAMOUS GUEST LEAVING SO SOON?
COULD HE REALLY BE SHUNNING THE OPPORTUNITY TO HAVE HIS BRILLIANT AND WITTY VOICE HEARD?
YOU FORGOT "CHARMING," MY DEAR, BUT I FORGIVE YOU.
MMMWAH.
GENTLEMEN, MY BOAT WAITS.
I'LL LEAVE YOU IN THE FINE, ERUDITE, AND CHARMING COMPANY OF BARONESS VON SUTTNER, IF YOU DON'T MIND.

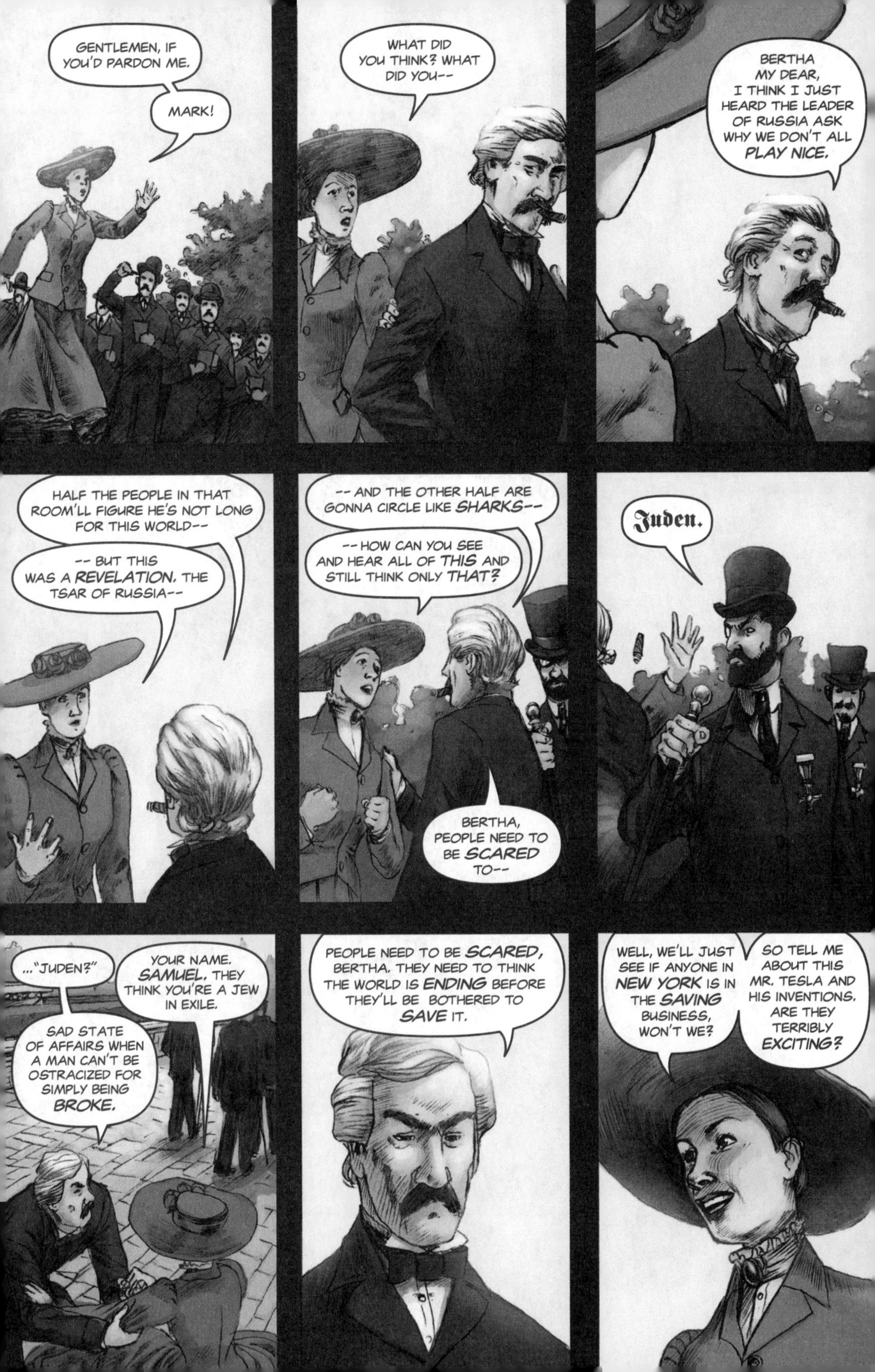
GENTLEMEN, IF YOU'D PARDON ME.
MARK!
WHAT DID YOU THINK? WHAT DID YOU--
BERTHA MY DEAR, I THINK I JUST HEARD THE LEADER OF RUSSIA ASK WHY WE DON'T ALL PLAY NICE.
HALF THE PEOPLE IN THAT ROOM'LL FIGURE HE'S NOT LONG FOR THIS WORLD--
-- BUT THIS WAS A REVELATION. THE TSAR OF RUSSIA--
-- AND THE OTHER HALF ARE GONNA CIRCLE LIKE SHARKS--
-- HOW CAN YOU SEE AND HEAR ALL OF THIS AND STILL THINK ONLY THAT?
BERTHA, PEOPLE NEED TO BE SCARED TO--
Juden.
..."JUDEN?"
YOUR NAME. SAMUEL. THEY THINK YOU'RE A JEW IN EXILE.
SAD STATE OF AFFAIRS WHEN A MAN CAN'T BE OSTRACIZED FOR SIMPLY BEING BROKE.
PEOPLE NEED TO BE SCARED, BERTHA. THEY NEED TO THINK THE WORLD IS ENDING BEFORE THEY'LL BE BOTHERED TO SAVE IT.
WELL, WE'LL JUST SEE IF ANYONE IN NEW YORK IS IN THE SAVING BUSINESS, WON'T WE?
SO TELL ME ABOUT THIS MR. TESLA AND HIS INVENTIONS. ARE THEY TERRIBLY EXCITING?

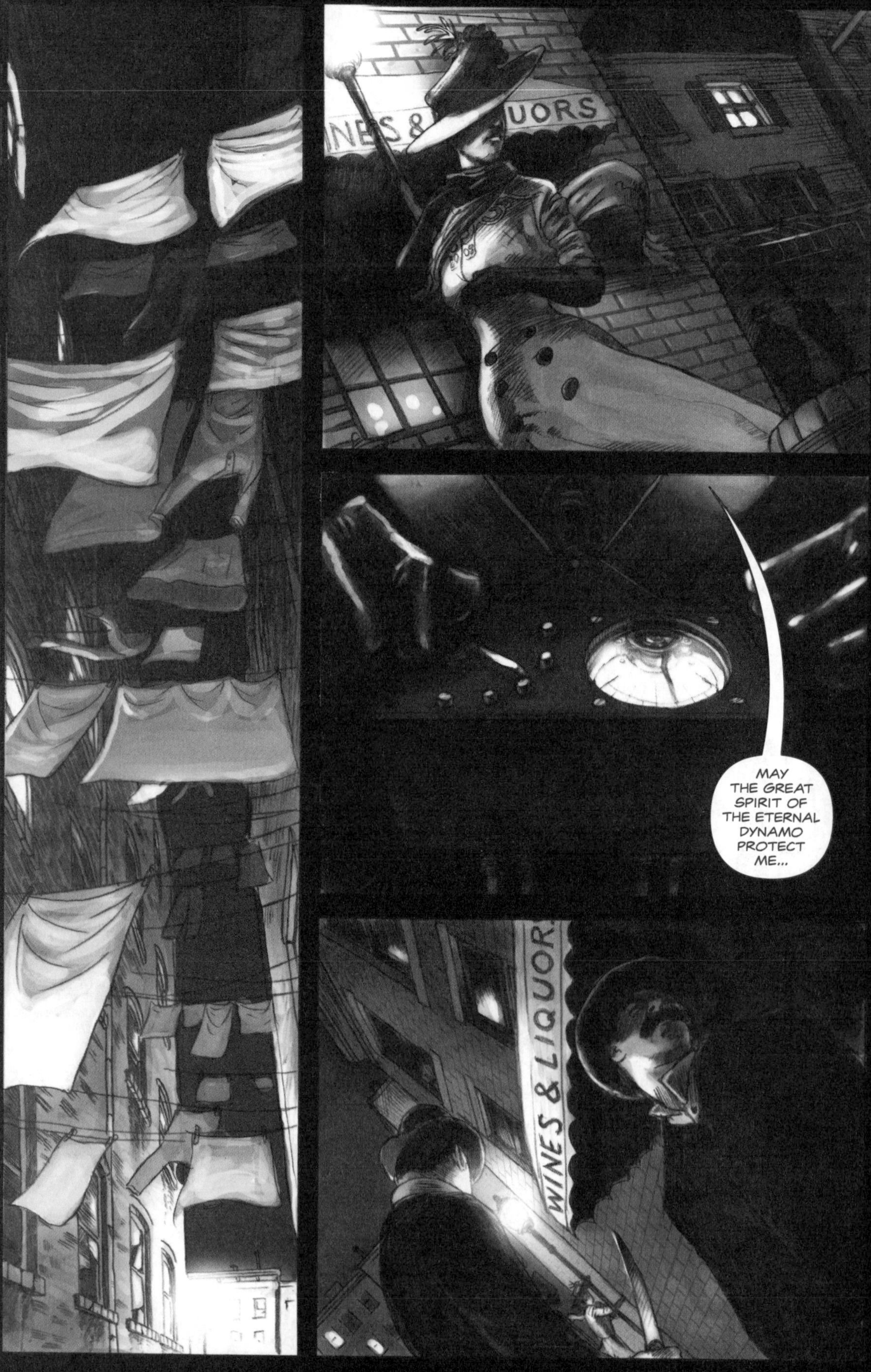

WINES & LIQUORS
MAY THE GREAT SPIRIT OF THE ETERNAL DYNAMO PROTECT ME...
WINES & LIQUORS

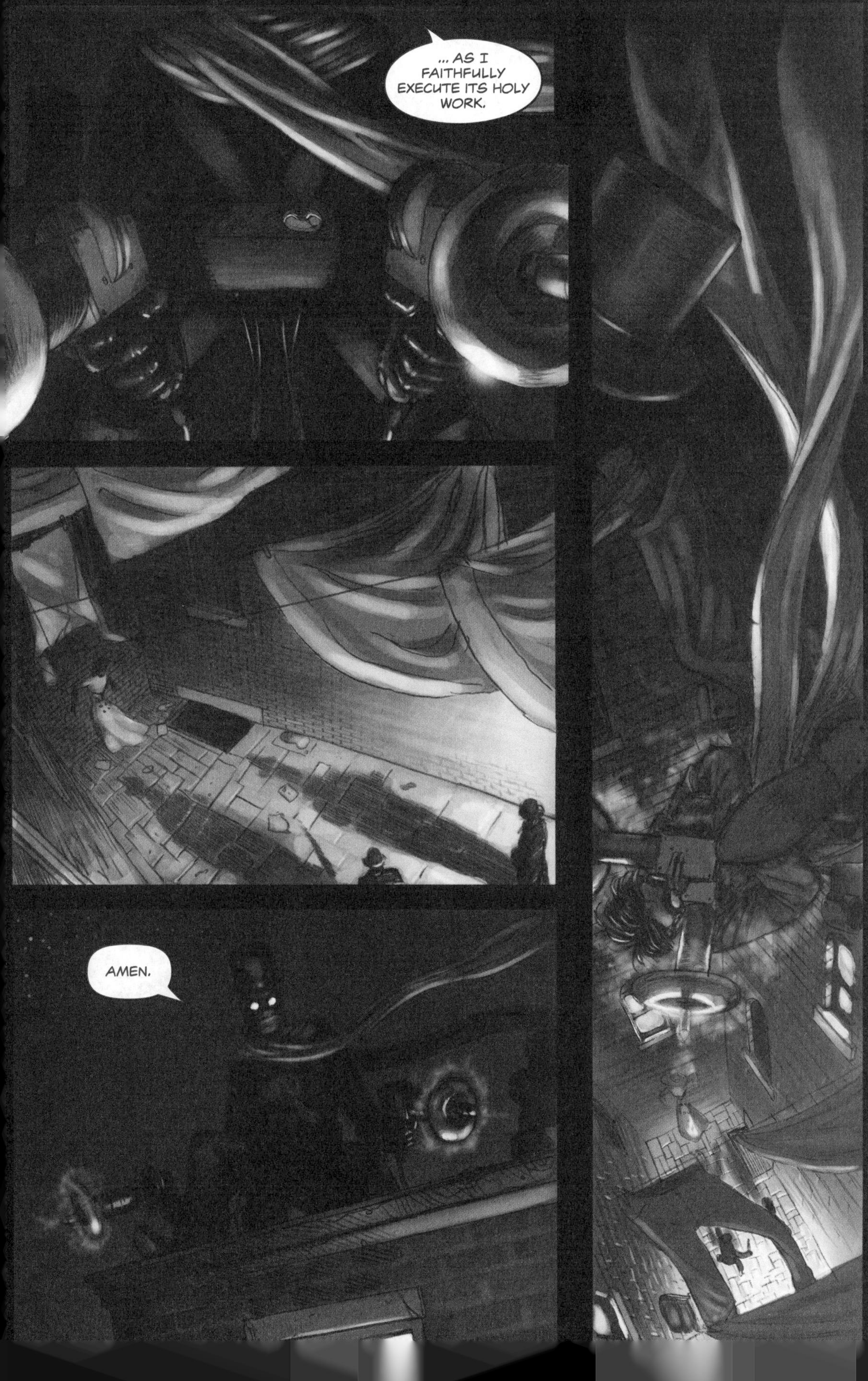
... AS I FAITHFULLY EXECUTE ITS HOLY WORK.
AMEN.

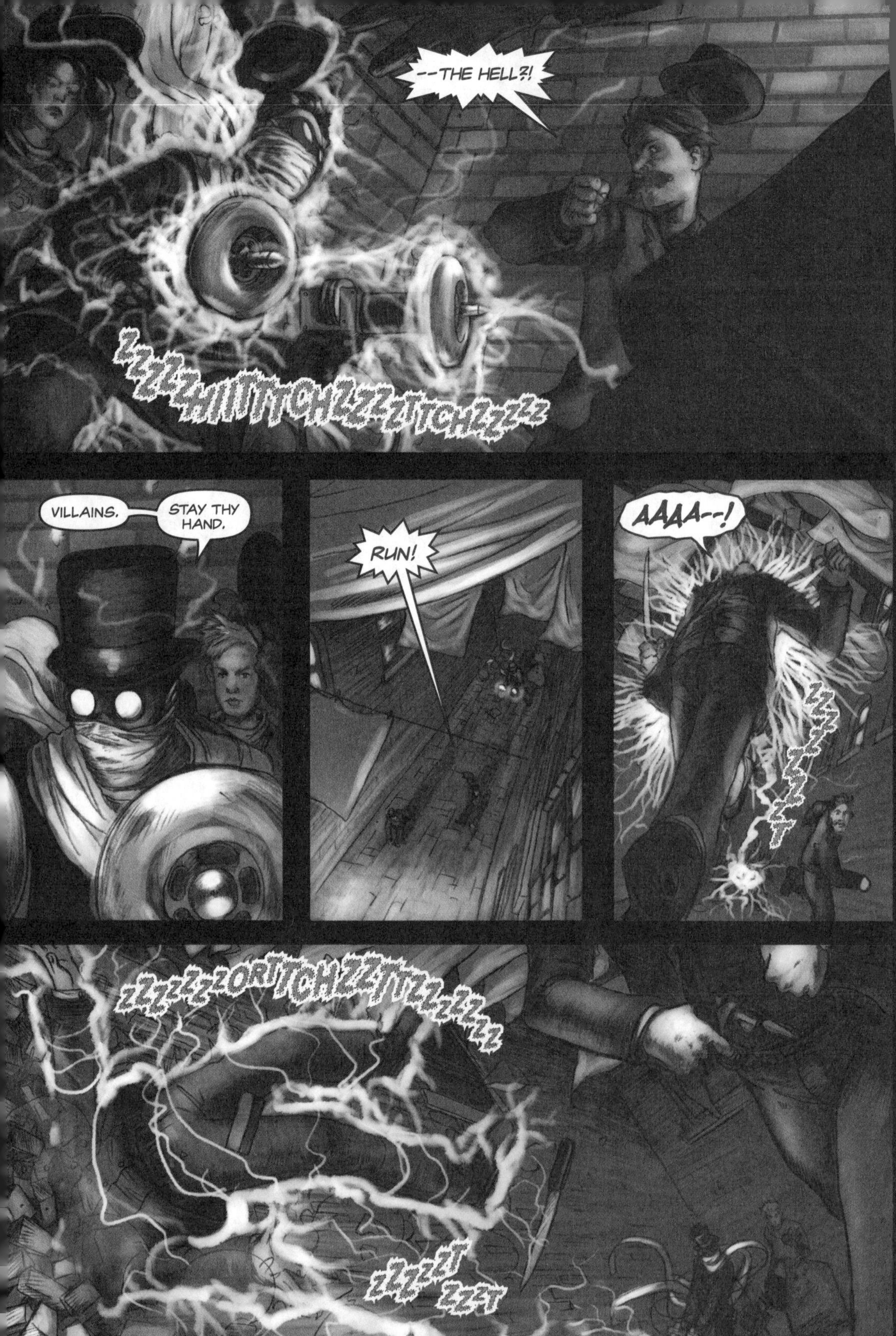
--THE HELL?!
ZZZZHIIITTTCHZZZZITCHZZZZ
VILLAINS.
STAY THY HAND.
RUN!
AAAA--!
ZZZZZZORTTCHZZTTZZZZZZZ
ZZZZT
ZZZT

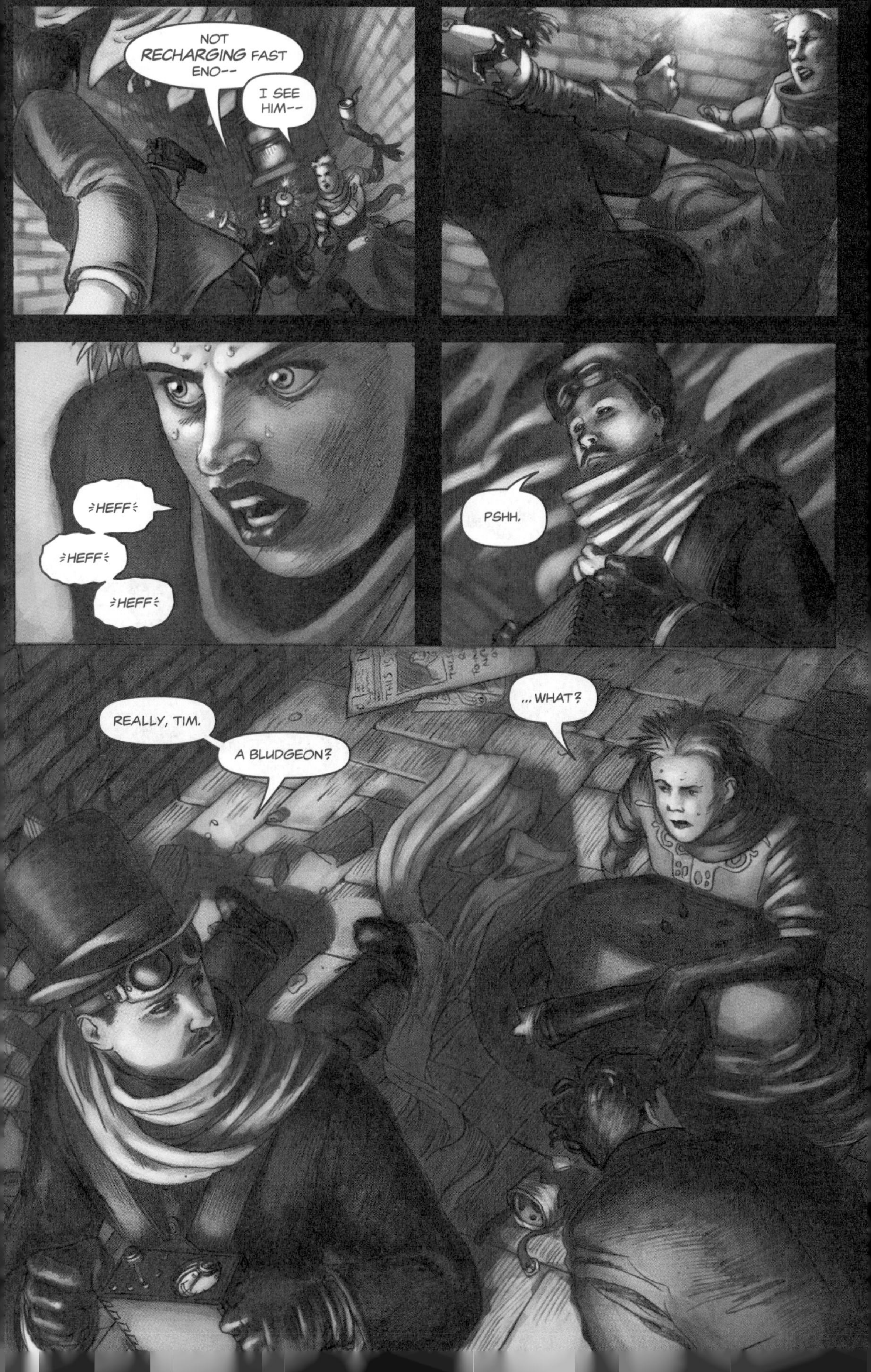
NOT RECHARGING FAST ENO--
I SEE HIM--
HEFF
HEFF
HEFF
PSHH.
REALLY, TIM.
A BLUDGEON?
...WHAT?

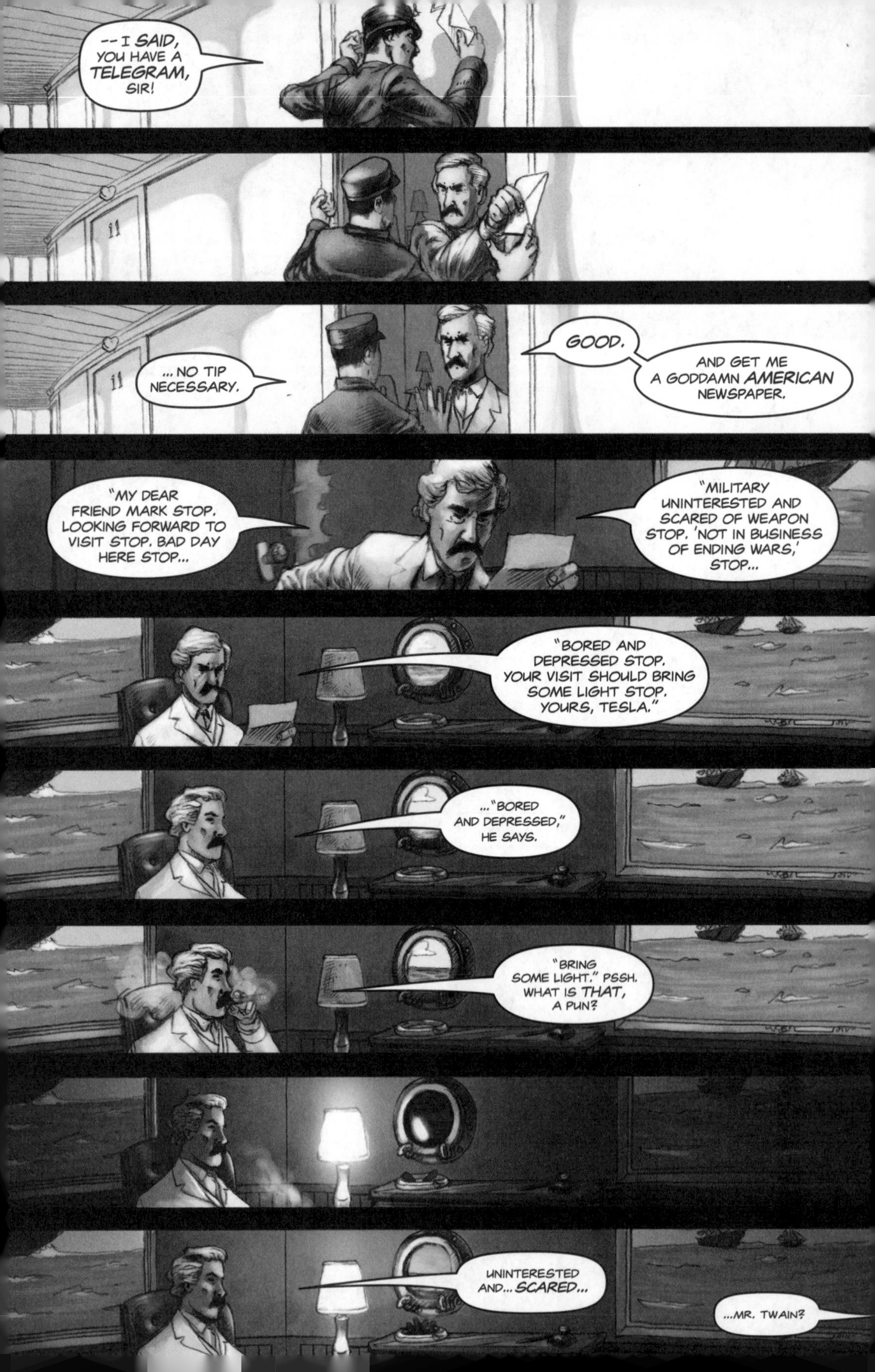
-- I SAID, YOU HAVE A TELEGRAM, SIR!
...NO TIP NECESSARY.
GOOD.
AND GET ME A GODDAMN AMERICAN NEWSPAPER.
"MY DEAR FRIEND MARK STOP. LOOKING FORWARD TO VISIT STOP. BAD DAY HERE STOP...
"MILITARY UNINTERESTED AND SCARED OF WEAPON STOP. 'NOT IN BUSINESS OF ENDING WARS,' STOP...
"BORED AND DEPRESSED STOP. YOUR VISIT SHOULD BRING SOME LIGHT STOP. YOURS, TESLA."
..."BORED AND DEPRESSED," HE SAYS.
"BRING SOME LIGHT." PSSH. WHAT IS THAT, A PUN?
UNINTERESTED AND... SCARED...
...MR. TWAIN?

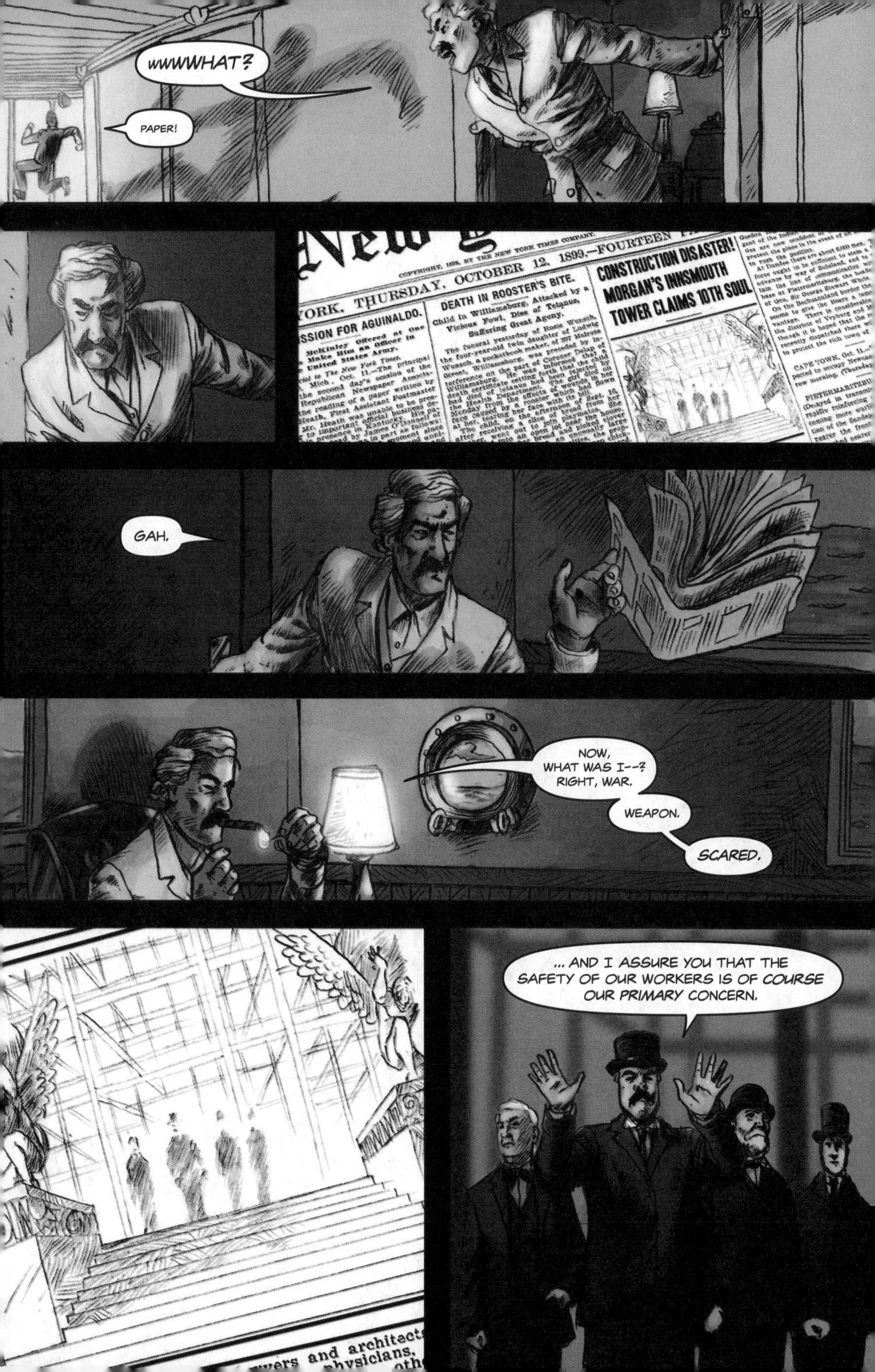
WWWHAT?
PAPER!
OCTOBER 12, 1899.
DEATH IN ROOSTER'S BITE.
CONSTRUCTION DISASTER!
MORGAN'S INNSMOUTH TOWER CLAIMS 10TH SOUL
GAH.
NOW, WHAT WAS I--? RIGHT, WAR.
WEAPON.
SCARED.
... AND I ASSURE YOU THAT THE SAFETY OF OUR WORKERS IS OF COURSE OUR PRIMARY CONCERN.

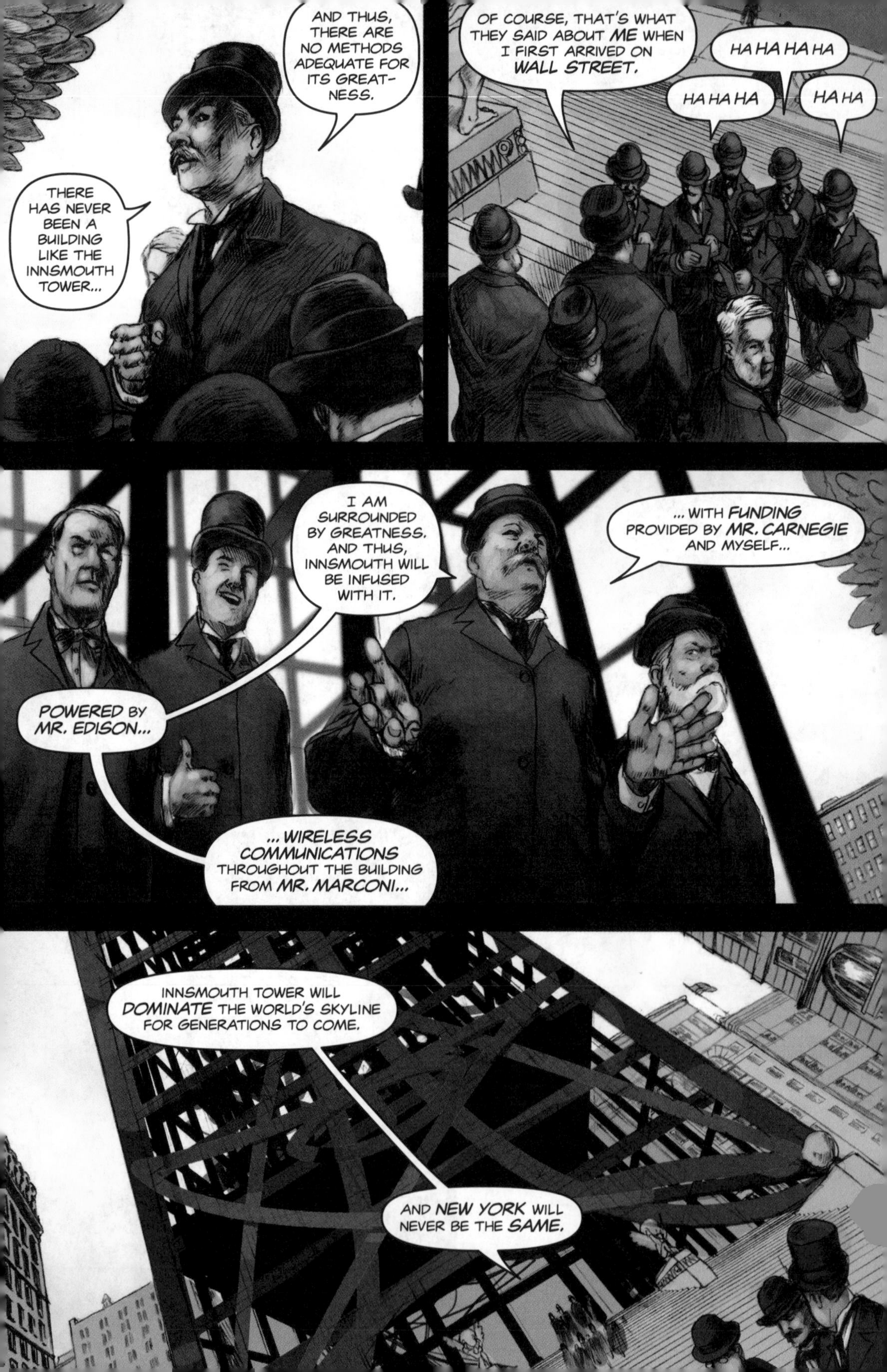
THERE HAS NEVER BEEN A BUILDING LIKE THE INNSMOUTH TOWER...
AND THUS, THERE ARE NO METHODS ADEQUATE FOR ITS GREATNESS.
OF COURSE, THAT'S WHAT THEY SAID ABOUT ME WHEN I FIRST ARRIVED ON WALL STREET.
HA HA HA HA
HA HA HA
HA HA
I AM SURROUNDED BY GREATNESS. AND THUS, INNSMOUTH WILL BE INFUSED WITH IT.
POWERED BY MR. EDISON...
...WIRELESS COMMUNICATIONS THROUGHOUT THE BUILDING FROM MR. MARCONI...
...WITH FUNDING PROVIDED BY MR. CARNEGIE AND MYSELF...
INNSMOUTH TOWER WILL DOMINATE THE WORLD'S SKYLINE FOR GENERATIONS TO COME.
AND NEW YORK WILL NEVER BE THE SAME.

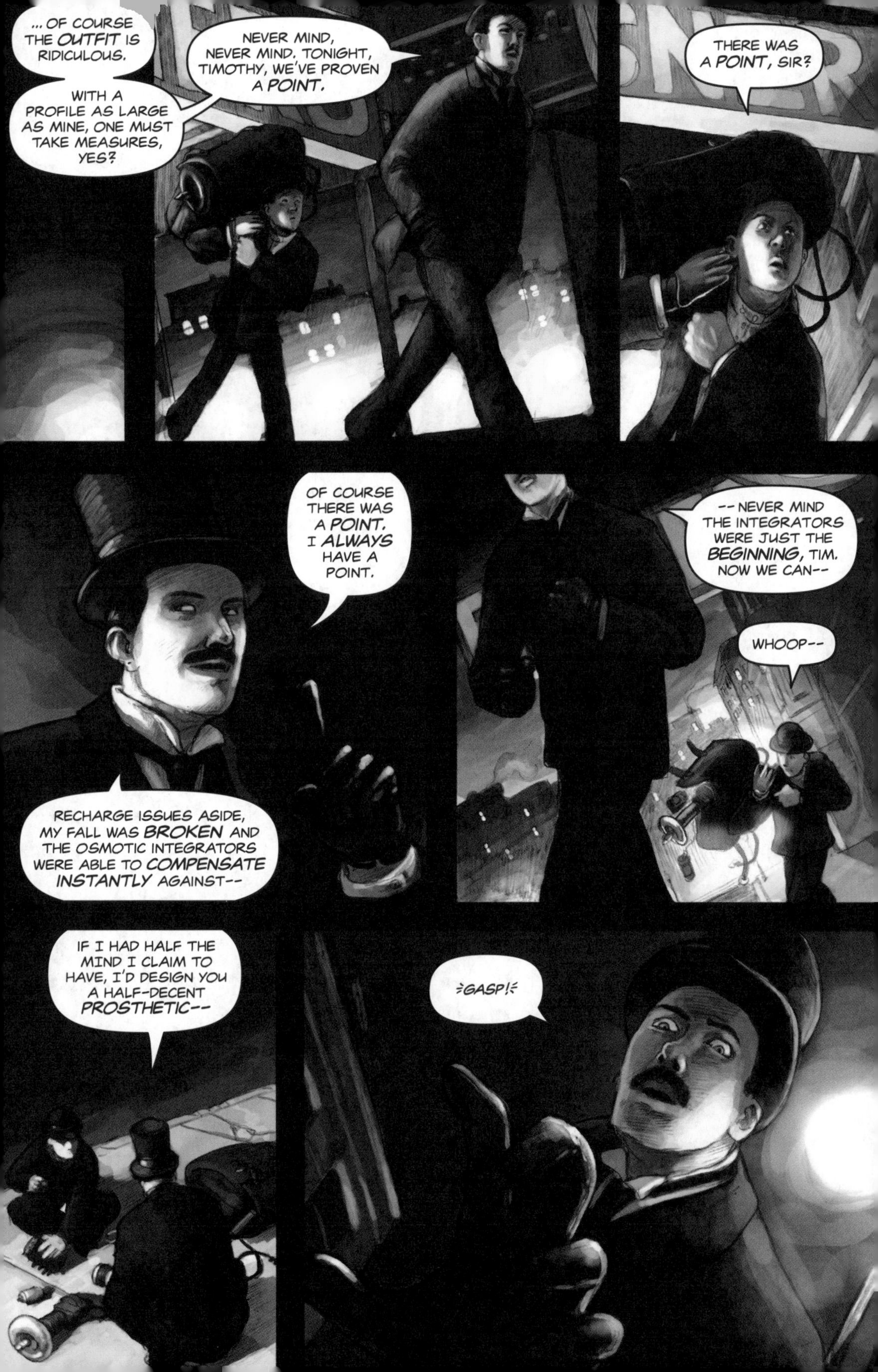
...OF COURSE THE OUTFIT IS RIDICULOUS.
WITH A PROFILE AS LARGE AS MINE, ONE MUST TAKE MEASURES, YES?
NEVER MIND, NEVER MIND. TONIGHT, TIMOTHY, WE'VE PROVEN A POINT.
THERE WAS A POINT, SIR?
OF COURSE THERE WAS A POINT. I ALWAYS HAVE A POINT.
RECHARGE ISSUES ASIDE, MY FALL WAS BROKEN AND THE OSMOTIC INTEGRATORS WERE ABLE TO COMPENSATE INSTANTLY AGAINST--
--NEVER MIND THE INTEGRATORS WERE JUST THE BEGINNING, TIM. NOW WE CAN--
WHOOP--
IF I HAD HALF THE MIND I CLAIM TO HAVE, I'D DESIGN YOU A HALF-DECENT PROSTHETIC--
GASP!

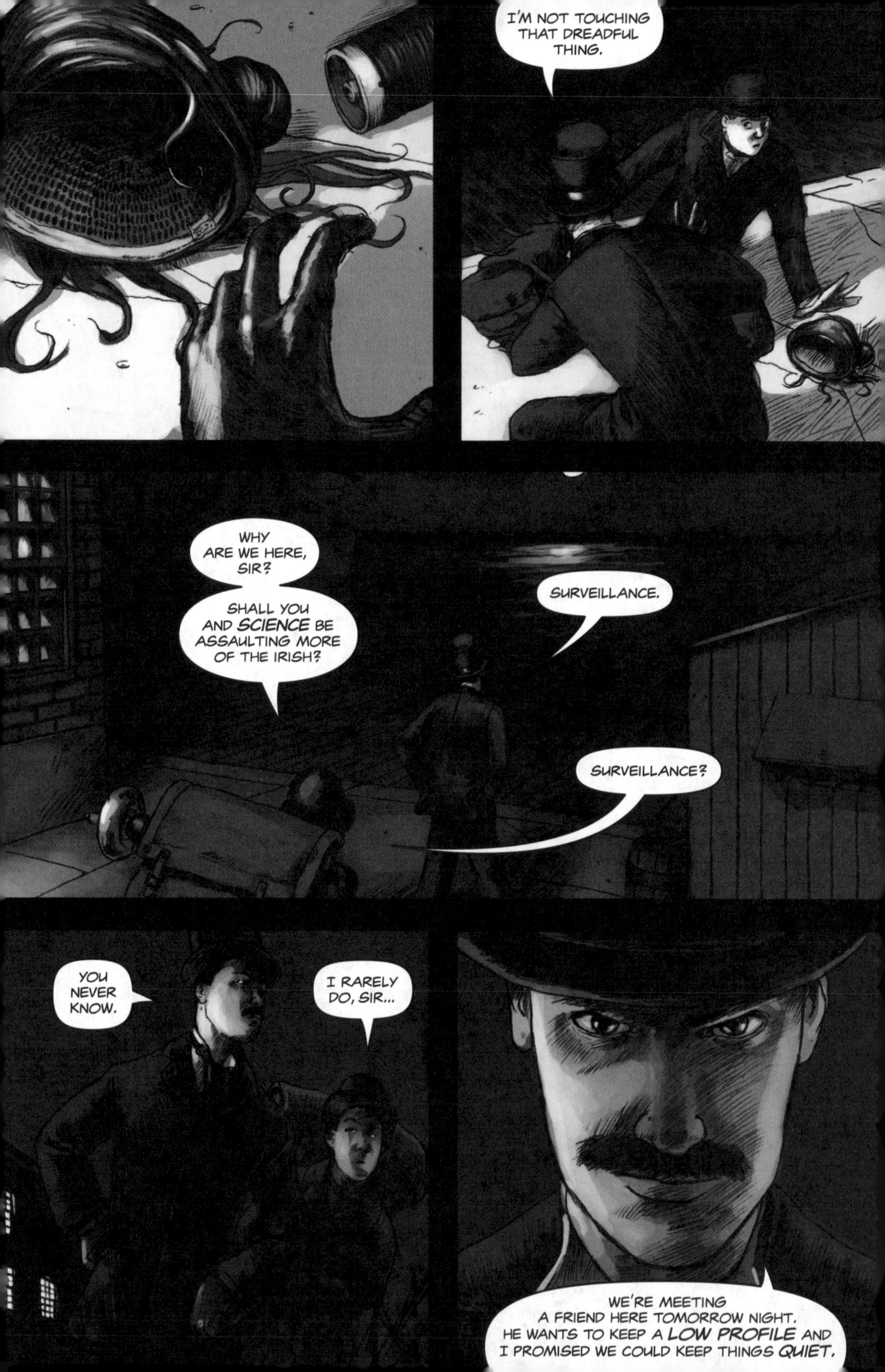

I'M NOT TOUCHING THAT DREADFUL THING.
WHY ARE WE HERE, SIR?
SHALL YOU AND SCIENCE BE ASSAULTING MORE OF THE IRISH?
SURVEILLANCE.
SURVEILLANCE?
YOU NEVER KNOW.
I RARELY DO, SIR...
WE'RE MEETING A FRIEND HERE TOMORROW NIGHT. HE WANTS TO KEEP A LOW PROFILE AND I PROMISED WE COULD KEEP THINGS QUIET.

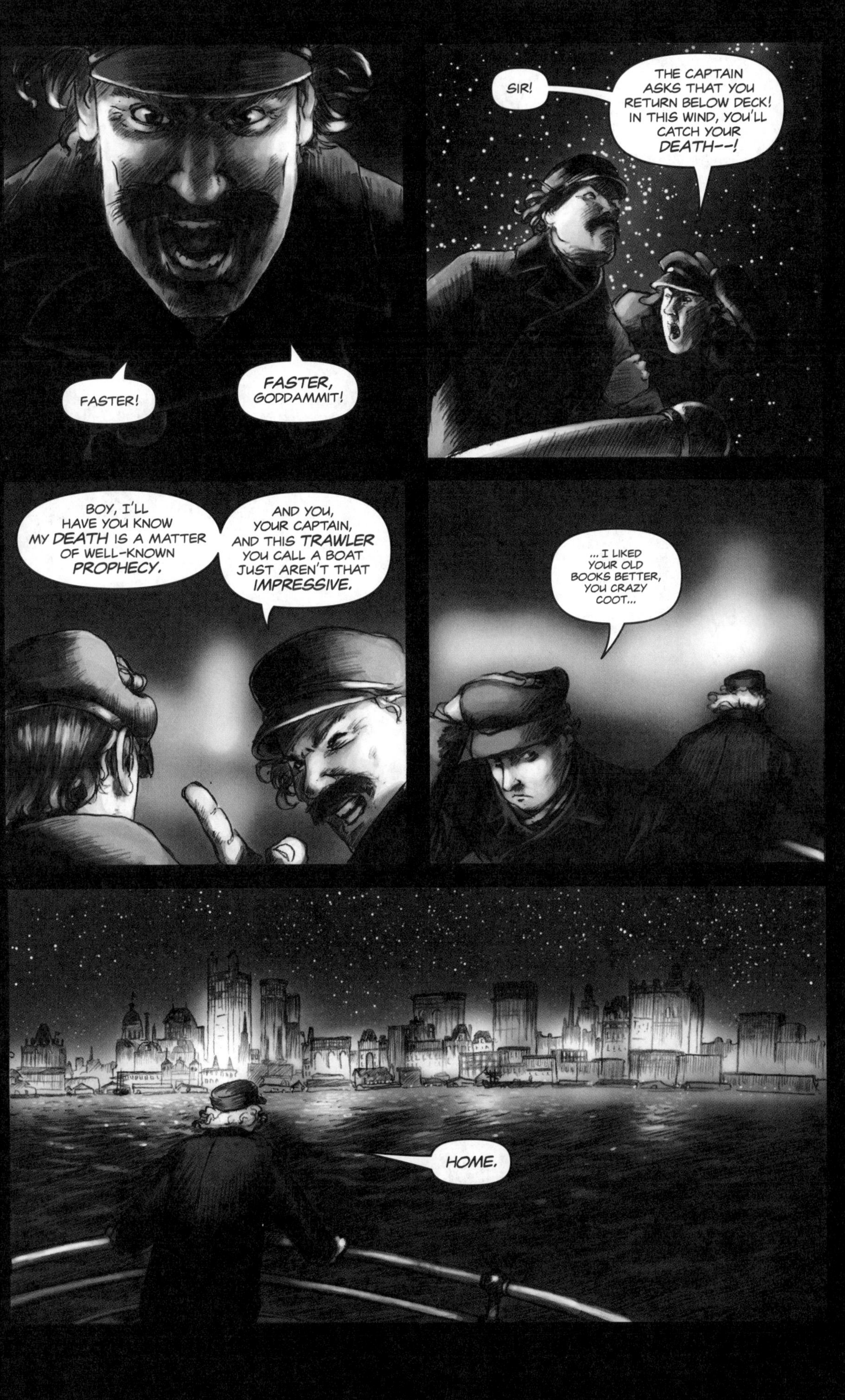
FASTER!
FASTER, GODDAMMIT!
SIR!
THE CAPTAIN ASKS THAT YOU RETURN BELOW DECK! IN THIS WIND, YOU'LL CATCH YOUR DEATH--!
BOY, I'LL HAVE YOU KNOW MY DEATH IS A MATTER OF WELL-KNOWN PROPHECY.
AND YOU, YOUR CAPTAIN, AND THIS TRAWLER YOU CALL A BOAT JUST AREN'T THAT IMPRESSIVE.
... I LIKED YOUR OLD BOOKS BETTER, YOU CRAZY COOT...
HOME.

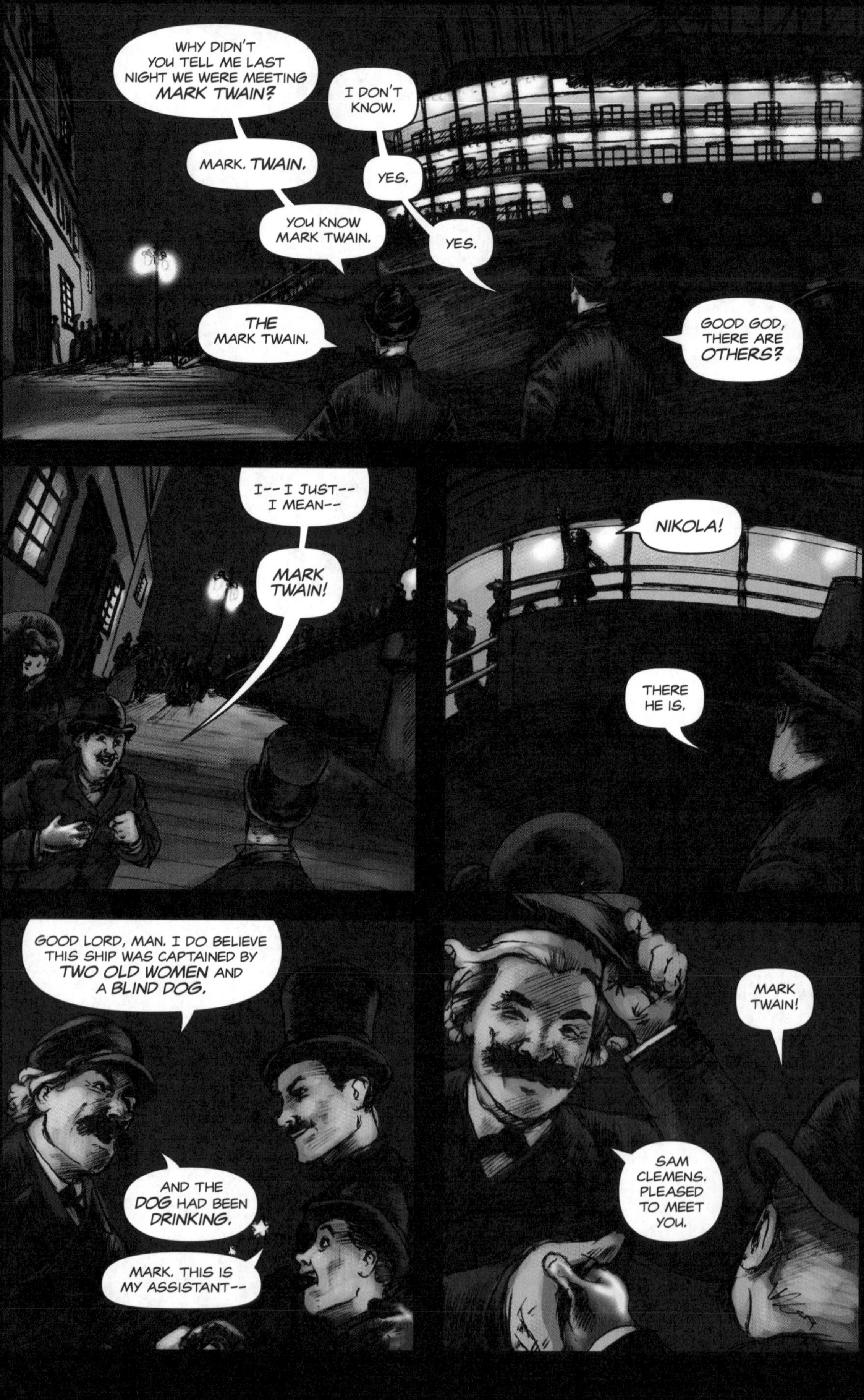
WHY DIDN'T YOU TELL ME LAST NIGHT WE WERE MEETING MARK TWAIN?
I DON'T KNOW.
MARK. TWAIN.
YES.
YOU KNOW MARK TWAIN.
YES.
THE MARK TWAIN.
GOOD GOD, THERE ARE OTHERS?
I-- I JUST-- I MEAN--
MARK TWAIN!
NIKOLA!
THERE HE IS.
GOOD LORD, MAN. I DO BELIEVE THIS SHIP WAS CAPTAINED BY TWO OLD WOMEN AND A BLIND DOG.
AND THE DOG HAD BEEN DRINKING.
MARK. THIS IS MY ASSISTANT--
MARK TWAIN!
SAM CLEMENS. PLEASED TO MEET YOU.

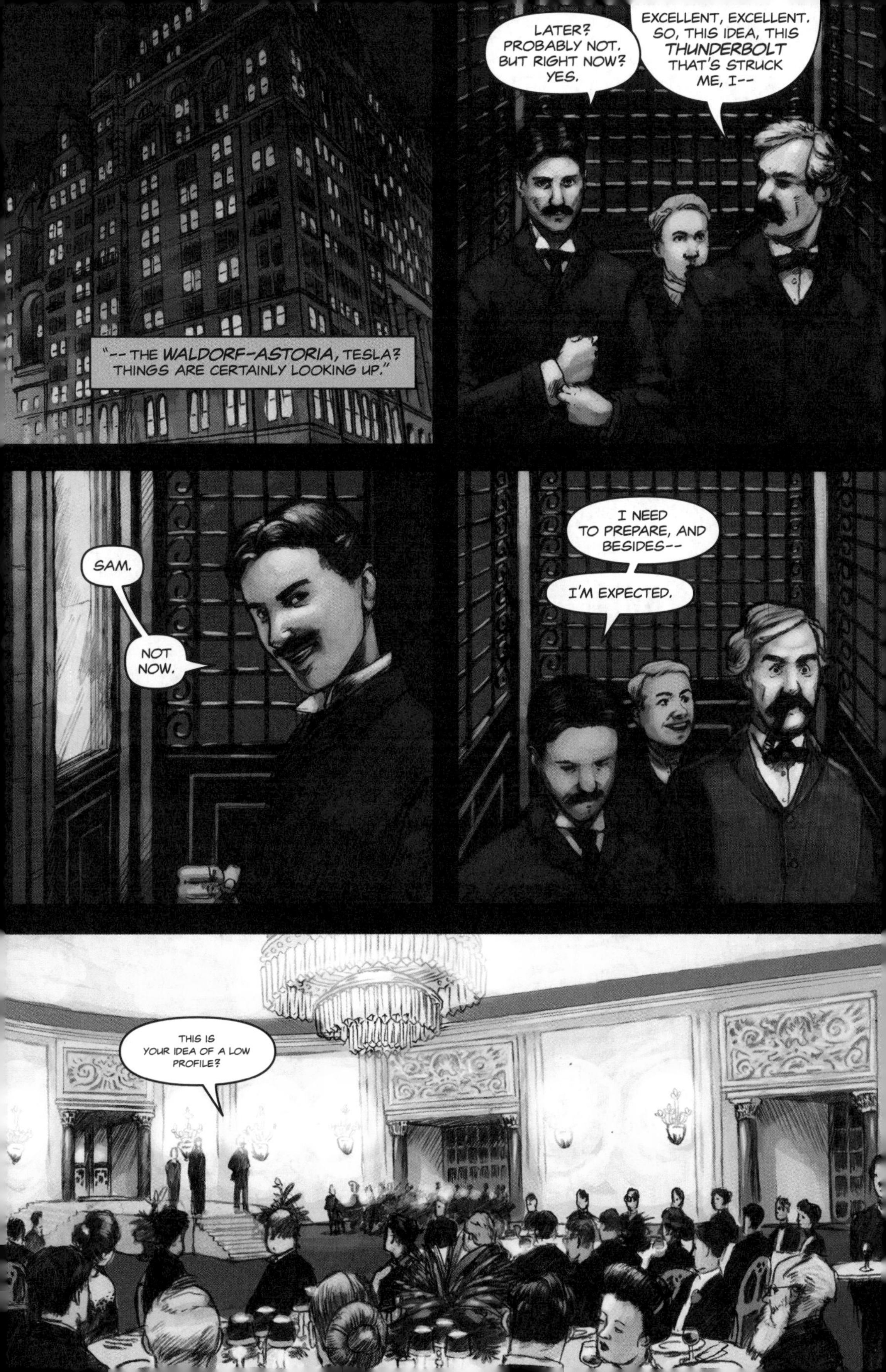
"-- THE WALDORF-ASTORIA, TESLA? THINGS ARE CERTAINLY LOOKING UP."
LATER? PROBABLY NOT. BUT RIGHT NOW? YES.
EXCELLENT, EXCELLENT. SO, THIS IDEA, THIS THUNDERBOLT THAT'S STRUCK ME, I--
SAM.
NOT NOW.
I NEED TO PREPARE, AND BESIDES--
I'M EXPECTED.
THIS IS YOUR IDEA OF A LOW PROFILE?

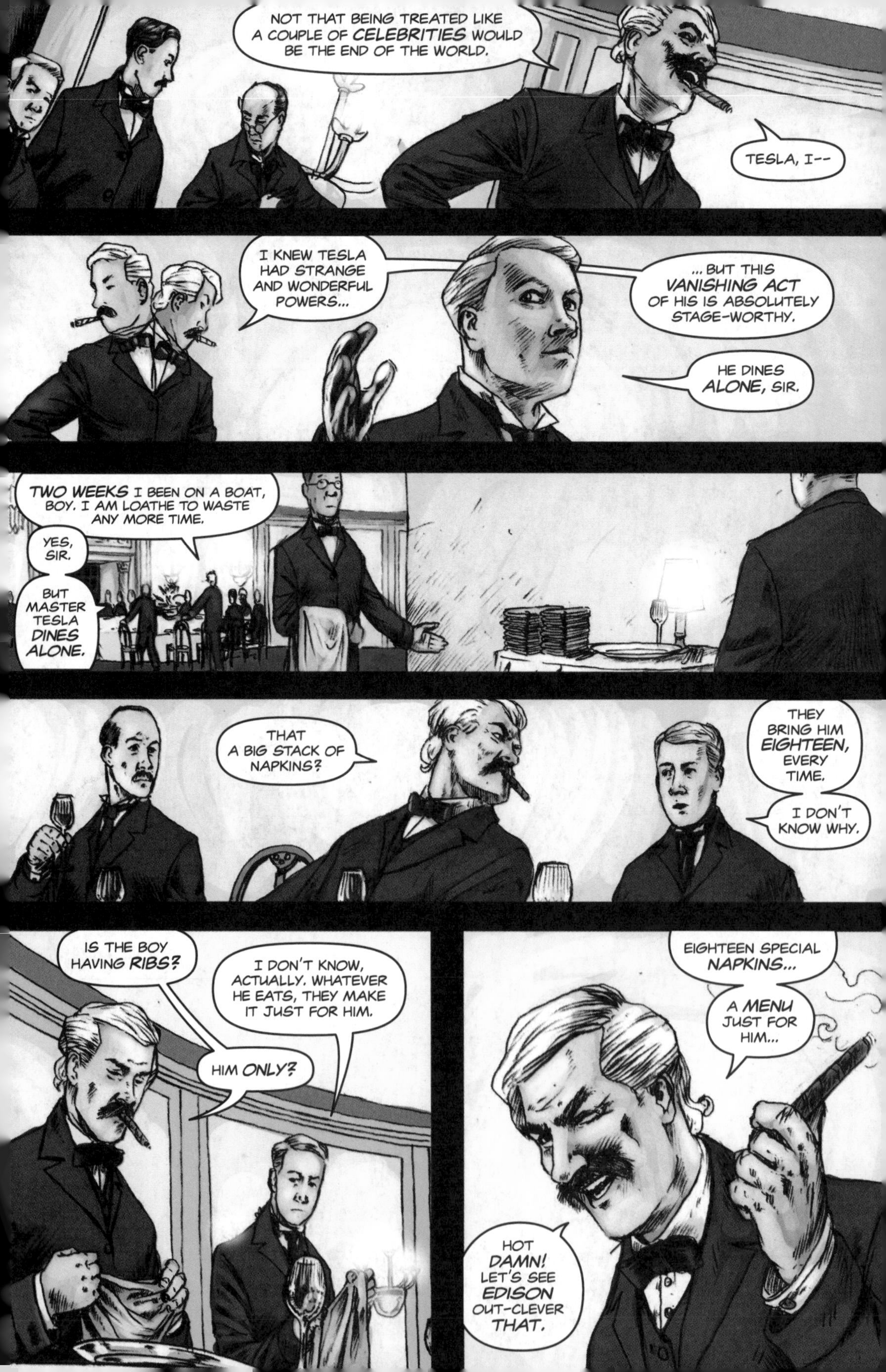
NOT THAT BEING TREATED LIKE A COUPLE OF CELEBRITIES WOULD BE THE END OF THE WORLD.
TESLA, I--
I KNEW TESLA HAD STRANGE AND WONDERFUL POWERS...
... BUT THIS VANISHING ACT OF HIS IS ABSOLUTELY STAGE-WORTHY.
HE DINES ALONE, SIR.
TWO WEEKS I BEEN ON A BOAT, BOY. I AM LOATHE TO WASTE ANY MORE TIME.
YES, SIR.
BUT MASTER TESLA DINES ALONE.
THAT A BIG STACK OF NAPKINS?
THEY BRING HIM EIGHTEEN, EVERY TIME.
I DON'T KNOW WHY.
IS THE BOY HAVING RIBS?
I DON'T KNOW, ACTUALLY. WHATEVER HE EATS, THEY MAKE IT JUST FOR HIM.
HIM ONLY?
EIGHTEEN SPECIAL NAPKINS...
A MENU JUST FOR HIM...
HOT DAMN! LET'S SEE EDISON OUT-CLEVER THAT.

IT WILL PASS HERE.

YOU'RE SURE?

HERE.

MY ANCESTORS HAVE LIVED IN THE SHADOW OF *ANNAPURNA* SINCE BEFORE YOURS COULD *SPEAK.* I KNOW THE *THORUNG LA* PASS AS I KNOW MY OWN *FACE.*

IF I SAY IT WILL PASS HERE, IT WILL PASS HERE, *MR. EDISON.*

AND YET NOW YOU SPEND YOUR DAYS *CHEWING OPIUM* AND *GIGGLING* AT *SNOW.*

YOUR ANCESTORS MUST BE *PROUD* TO BE *SOLD OUT* BY SUCH A FINE *SCION* OF THEIR LINEAGE.

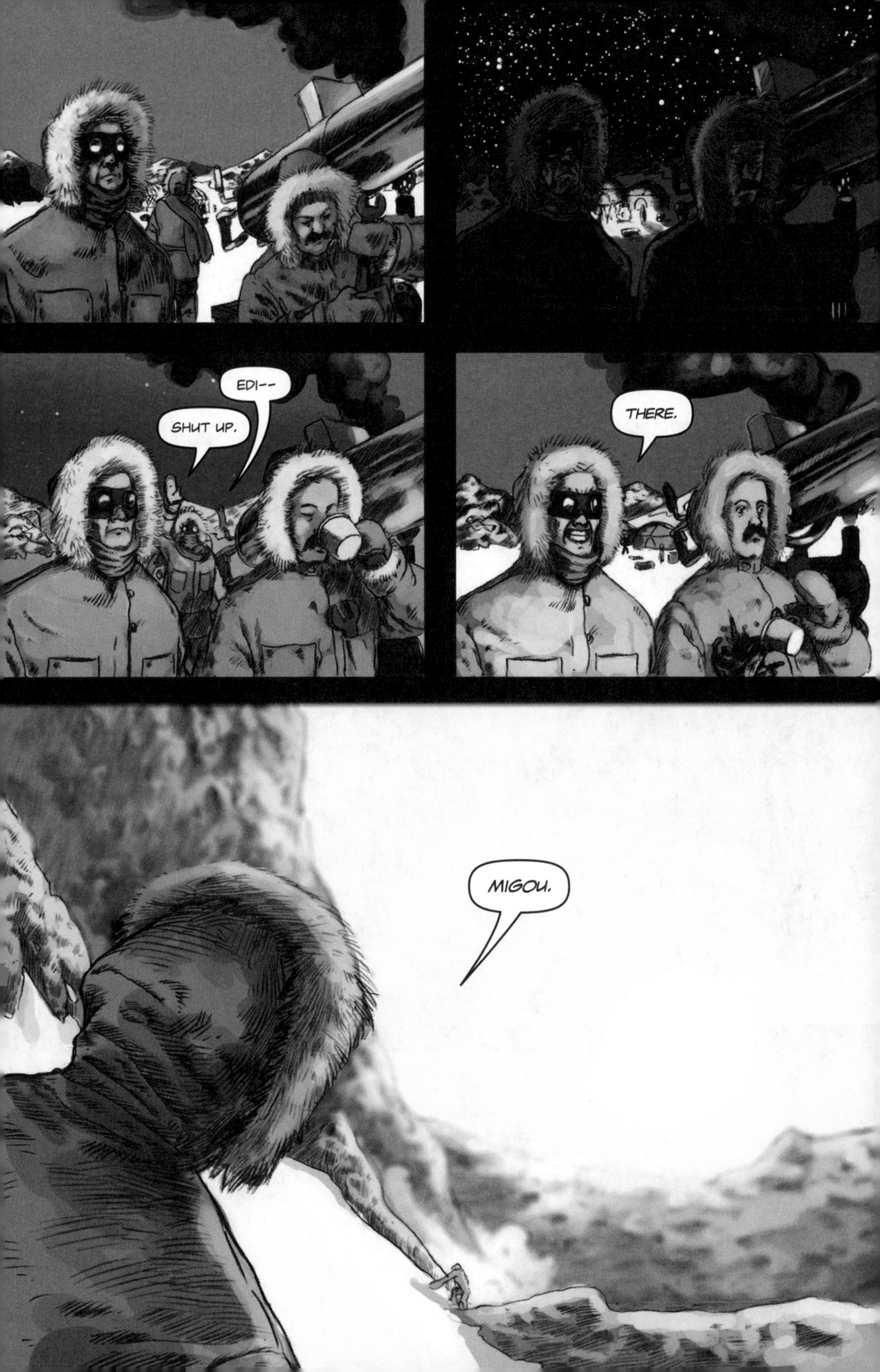
EDI--
SHUT UP.
THERE.
MIGOU.

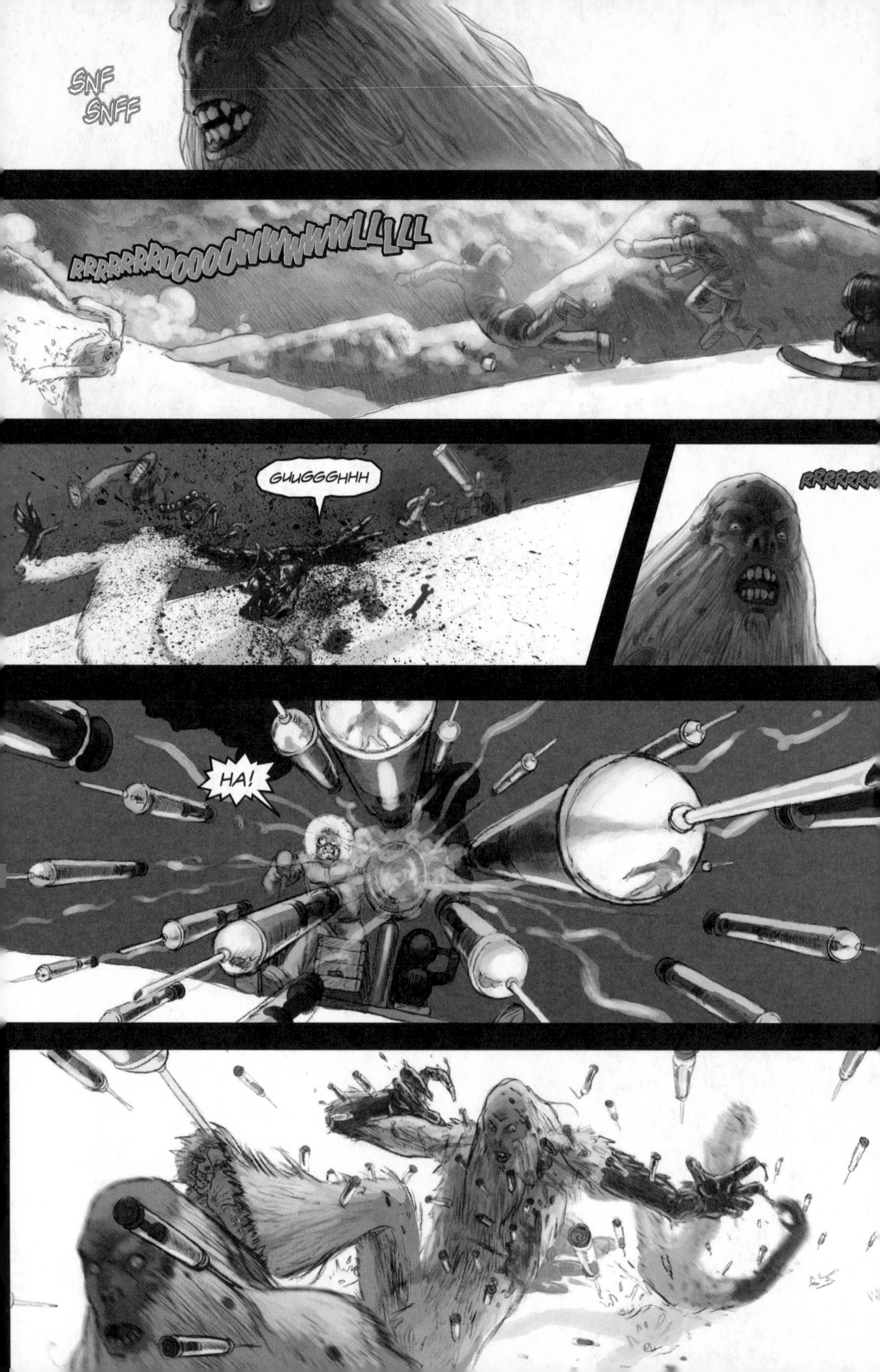
SNF
SNFF
RRRRRRROOOOOOWWWWWLLLLL
GUUGGGHHH
RRRRRR
HA!

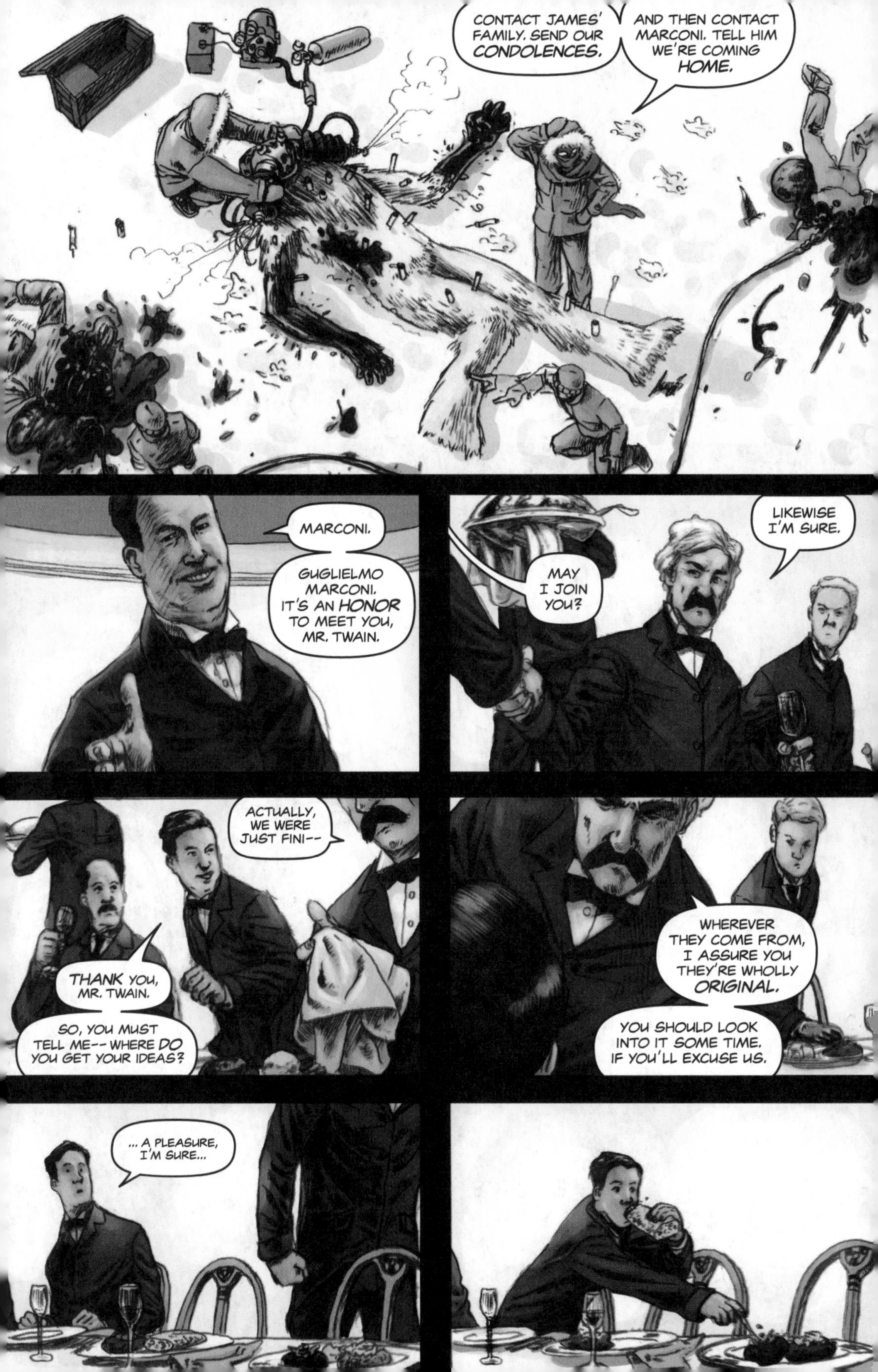
CONTACT JAMES' FAMILY. SEND OUR CONDOLENCES.
AND THEN CONTACT MARCONI. TELL HIM WE'RE COMING HOME.
MARCONI.
GUGLIELMO MARCONI. IT'S AN HONOR TO MEET YOU, MR. TWAIN.
MAY I JOIN YOU?
LIKEWISE I'M SURE.
ACTUALLY, WE WERE JUST FINI--
THANK YOU, MR. TWAIN.
SO, YOU MUST TELL ME-- WHERE DO YOU GET YOUR IDEAS?
WHEREVER THEY COME FROM, I ASSURE YOU THEY'RE WHOLLY ORIGINAL.
YOU SHOULD LOOK INTO IT SOME TIME. IF YOU'LL EXCUSE US.
... A PLEASURE, I'M SURE...

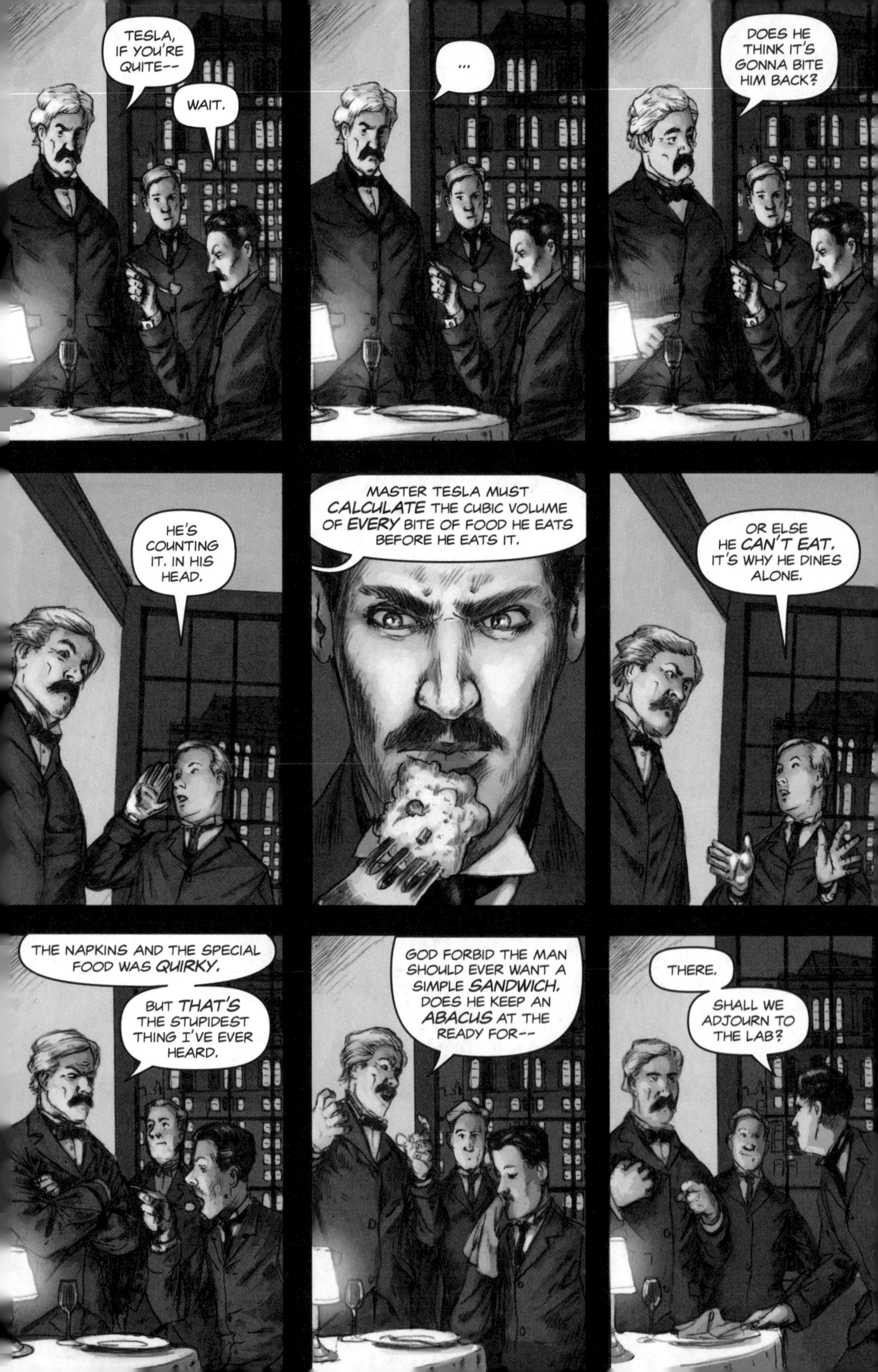
TESLA, IF YOU'RE QUITE--
WAIT.
...
DOES HE THINK IT'S GONNA BITE HIM BACK?
HE'S COUNTING IT. IN HIS HEAD.
MASTER TESLA MUST CALCULATE THE CUBIC VOLUME OF EVERY BITE OF FOOD HE EATS BEFORE HE EATS IT.
OR ELSE HE CAN'T EAT. IT'S WHY HE DINES ALONE.
THE NAPKINS AND THE SPECIAL FOOD WAS QUIRKY.
BUT THAT'S THE STUPIDEST THING I'VE EVER HEARD.
GOD FORBID THE MAN SHOULD EVER WANT A SIMPLE SANDWICH. DOES HE KEEP AN ABACUS AT THE READY FOR--
THERE.
SHALL WE ADJOURN TO THE LAB?

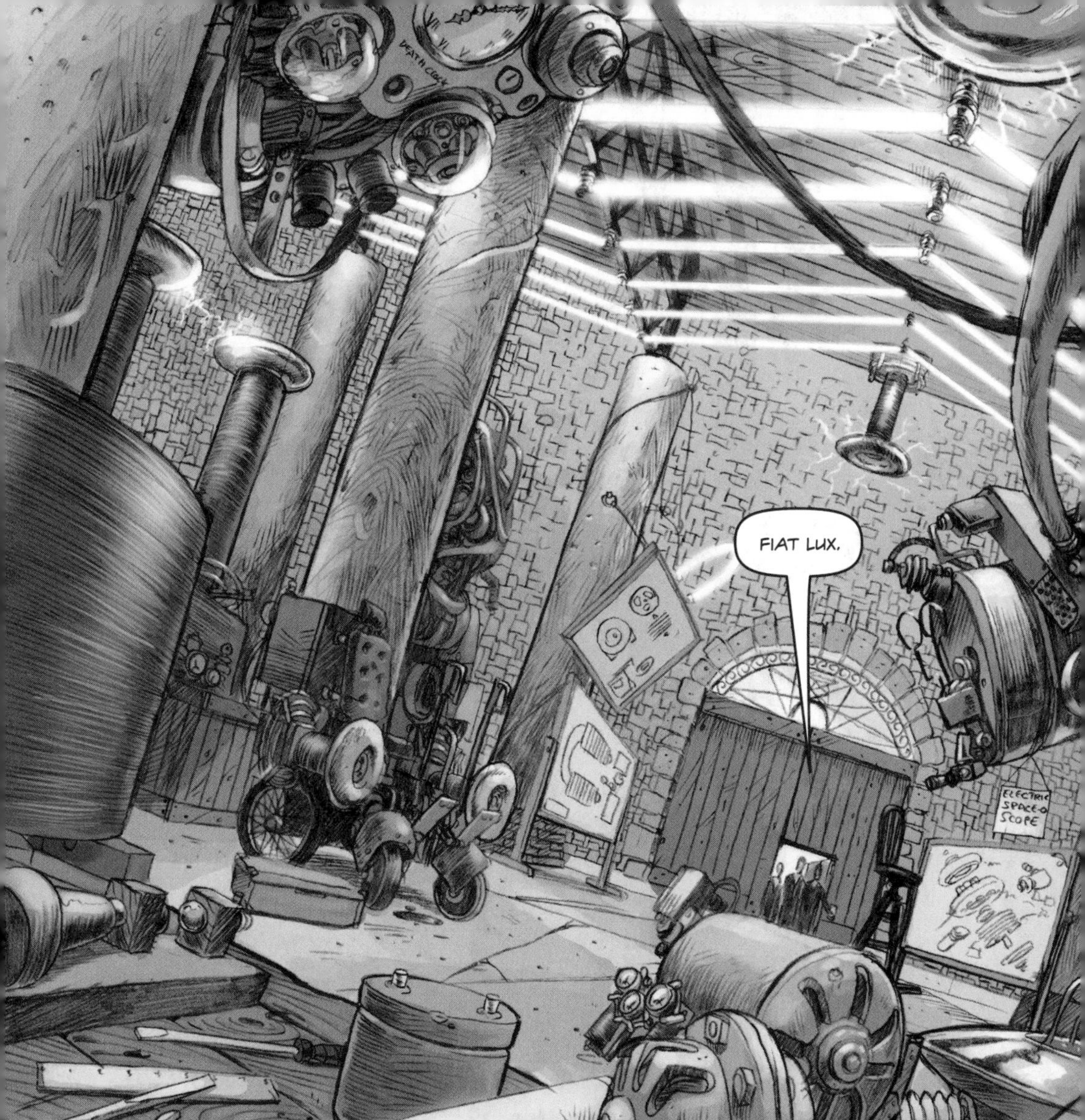
DEATH CLOCK
FIAT LUX.
ELECTRIC SPACE-O SCOPE

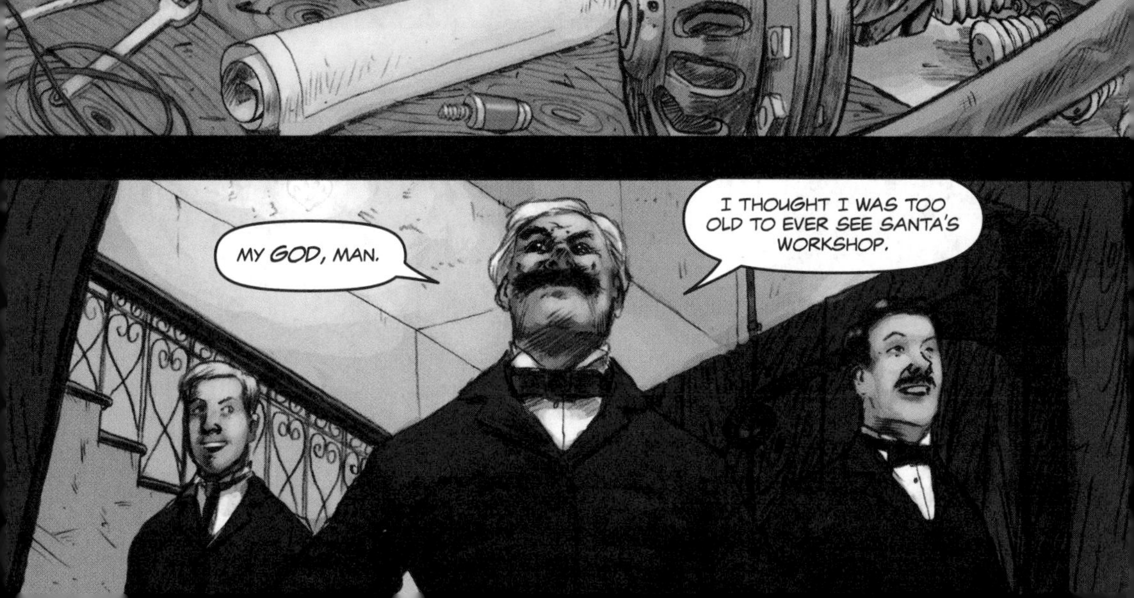
MY GOD, MAN.
I THOUGHT I WAS TOO OLD TO EVER SEE SANTA'S WORKSHOP.

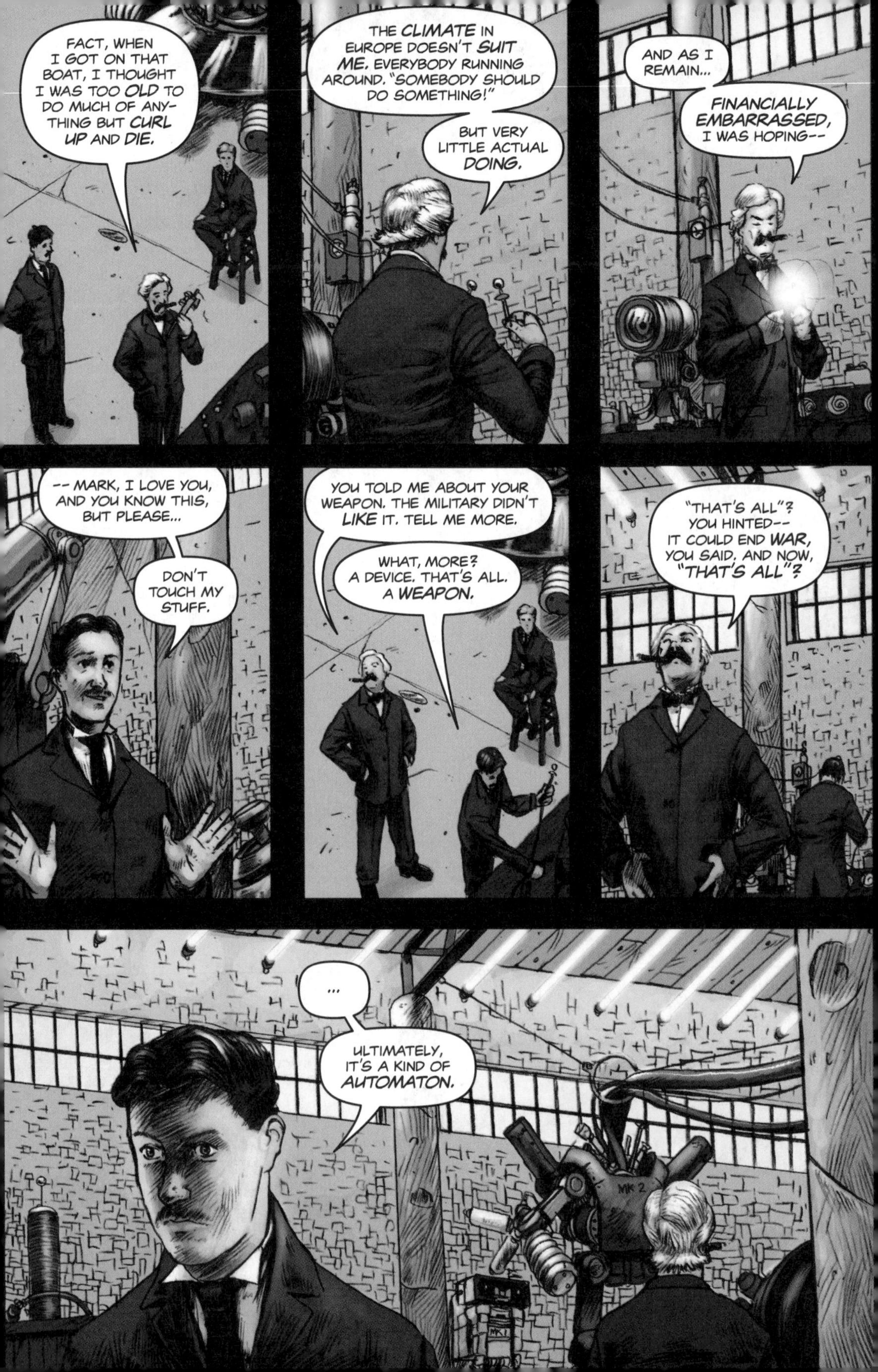
FACT, WHEN I GOT ON THAT BOAT, I THOUGHT I WAS TOO OLD TO DO MUCH OF ANY-THING BUT CURL UP AND DIE.
THE CLIMATE IN EUROPE DOESN'T SUIT ME. EVERYBODY RUNNING AROUND. "SOMEBODY SHOULD DO SOMETHING!"
BUT VERY LITTLE ACTUAL DOING.
AND AS I REMAIN...
FINANCIALLY EMBARRASSED, I WAS HOPING--
-- MARK, I LOVE YOU, AND YOU KNOW THIS, BUT PLEASE...
DON'T TOUCH MY STUFF.
YOU TOLD ME ABOUT YOUR WEAPON. THE MILITARY DIDN'T LIKE IT. TELL ME MORE.
WHAT, MORE? A DEVICE. THAT'S ALL. A WEAPON.
"THAT'S ALL"? YOU HINTED-- IT COULD END WAR, YOU SAID. AND NOW, "THAT'S ALL"?
...
ULTIMATELY, IT'S A KIND OF AUTOMATON.
MK 2

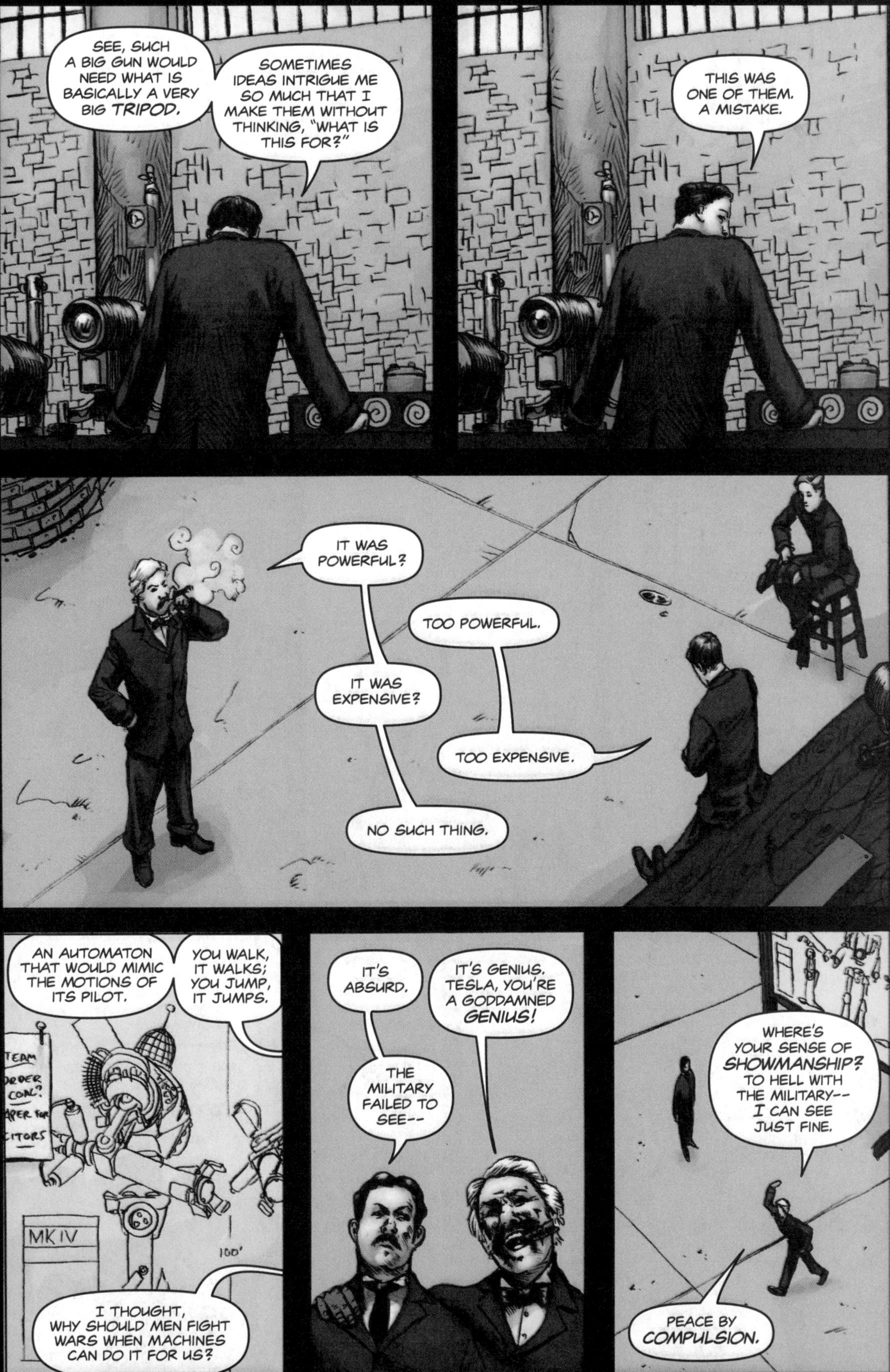
SEE, SUCH A BIG GUN WOULD NEED WHAT IS BASICALLY A VERY BIG TRIPOD.
SOMETIMES IDEAS INTRIGUE ME SO MUCH THAT I MAKE THEM WITHOUT THINKING, "WHAT IS THIS FOR?"
THIS WAS ONE OF THEM. A MISTAKE.
IT WAS POWERFUL?
TOO POWERFUL.
IT WAS EXPENSIVE?
TOO EXPENSIVE.
NO SUCH THING.
AN AUTOMATON THAT WOULD MIMIC THE MOTIONS OF ITS PILOT.
YOU WALK, IT WALKS; YOU JUMP, IT JUMPS.
MK IV
100'
I THOUGHT, WHY SHOULD MEN FIGHT WARS WHEN MACHINES CAN DO IT FOR US?
IT'S ABSURD.
IT'S GENIUS. TESLA, YOU'RE A GODDAMNED GENIUS!
THE MILITARY FAILED TO SEE--
WHERE'S YOUR SENSE OF SHOWMANSHIP? TO HELL WITH THE MILITARY-- I CAN SEE JUST FINE.
PEACE BY COMPULSION.

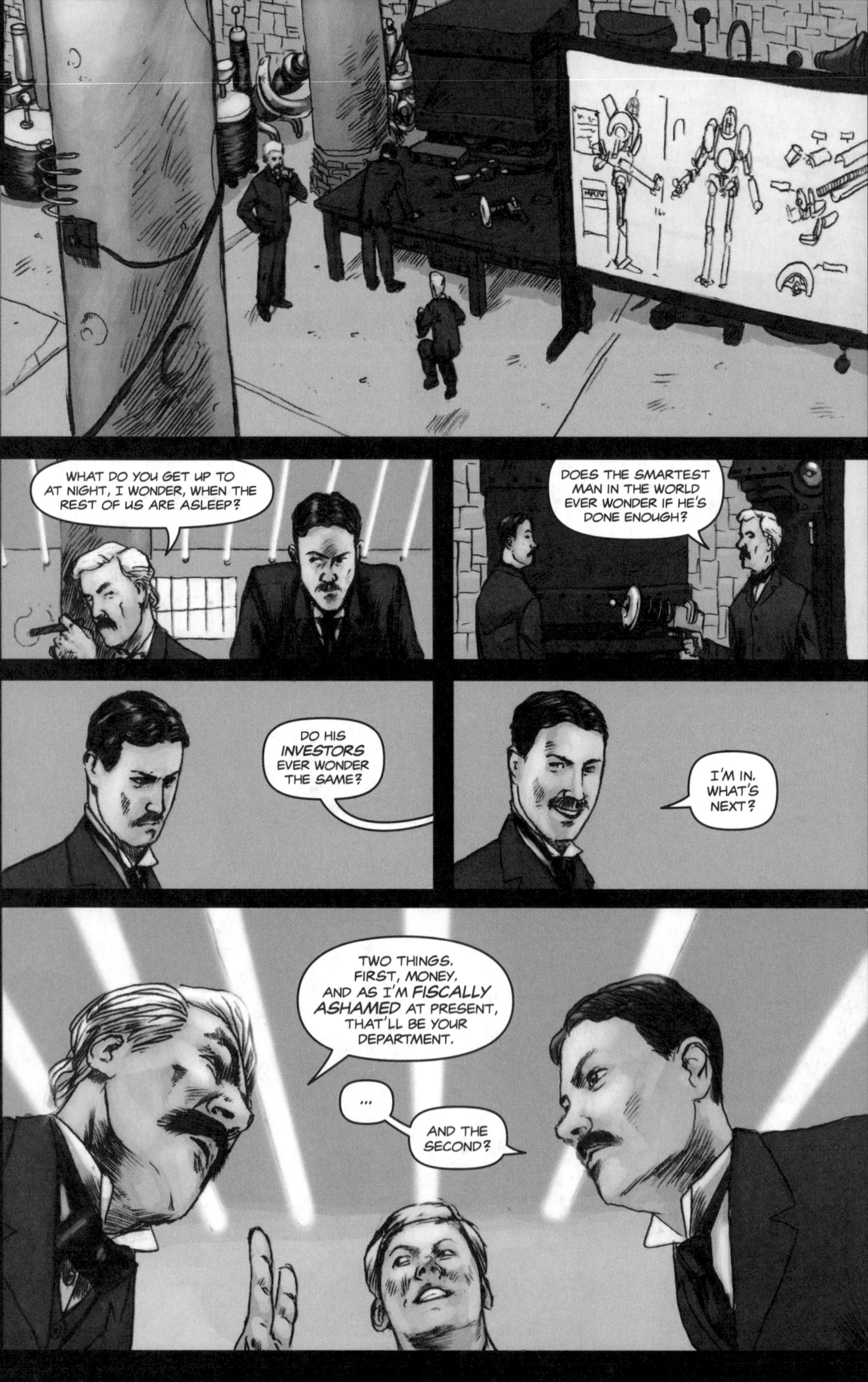
WHAT DO YOU GET UP TO AT NIGHT, I WONDER, WHEN THE REST OF US ARE ASLEEP?
DOES THE SMARTEST MAN IN THE WORLD EVER WONDER IF HE'S DONE ENOUGH?
DO HIS *INVESTORS* EVER WONDER THE SAME?
I'M IN. WHAT'S NEXT?
TWO THINGS. FIRST, MONEY. AND AS I'M *FISCALLY ASHAMED* AT PRESENT, THAT'LL BE YOUR DEPARTMENT.
...
AND THE SECOND?

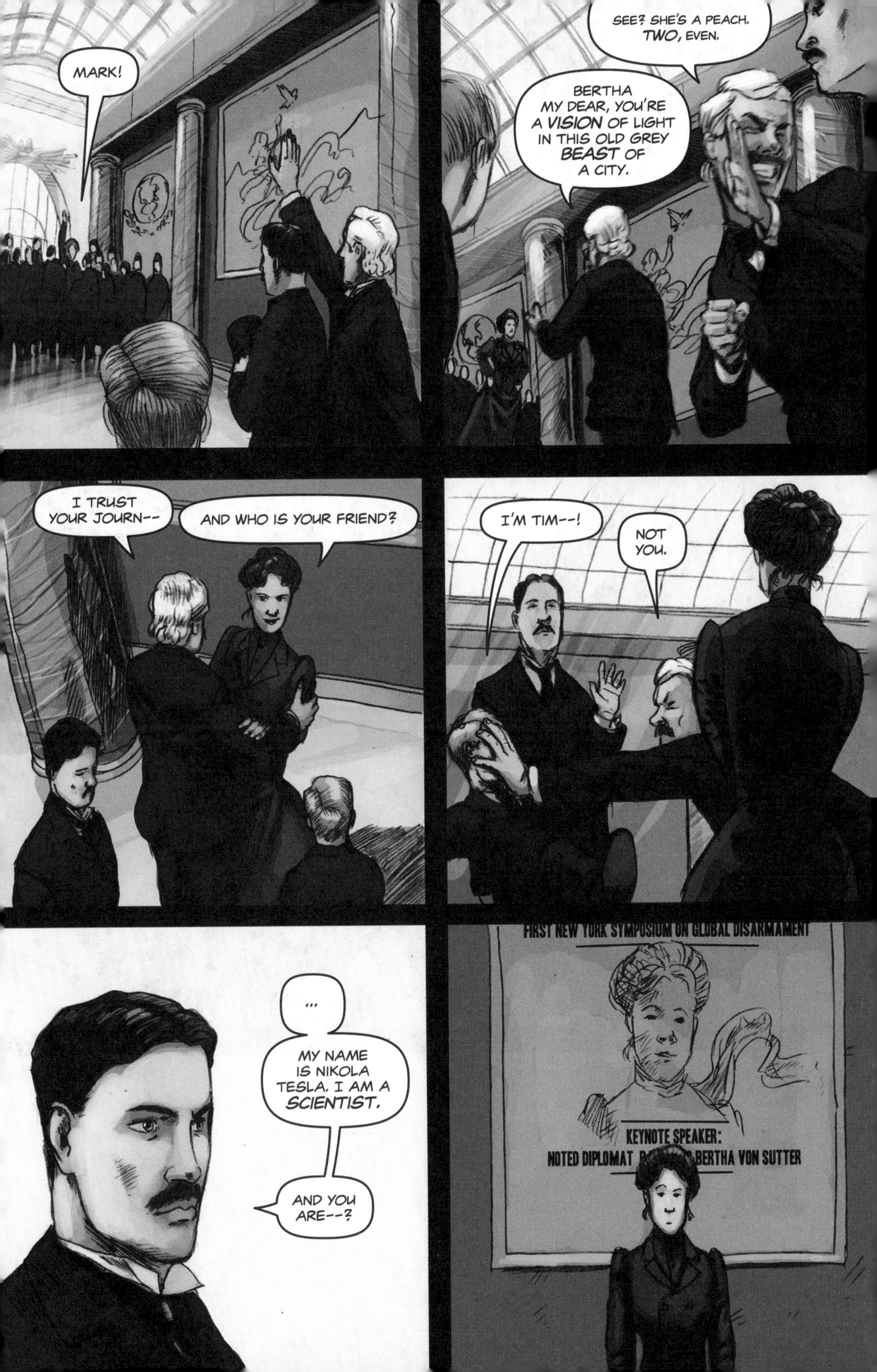
MARK!
SEE? SHE'S A PEACH. TWO, EVEN.
BERTHA MY DEAR, YOU'RE A VISION OF LIGHT IN THIS OLD GREY BEAST OF A CITY.
I TRUST YOUR JOURN--
AND WHO IS YOUR FRIEND?
I'M TIM--!
NOT YOU.
...
MY NAME IS NIKOLA TESLA. I AM A SCIENTIST.
AND YOU ARE--?
FIRST NEW YORK SYMPOSIUM ON GLOBAL DISARMAMENT
KEYNOTE SPEAKER:
NOTED DIPLOMAT
BERTHA VON SUTTER

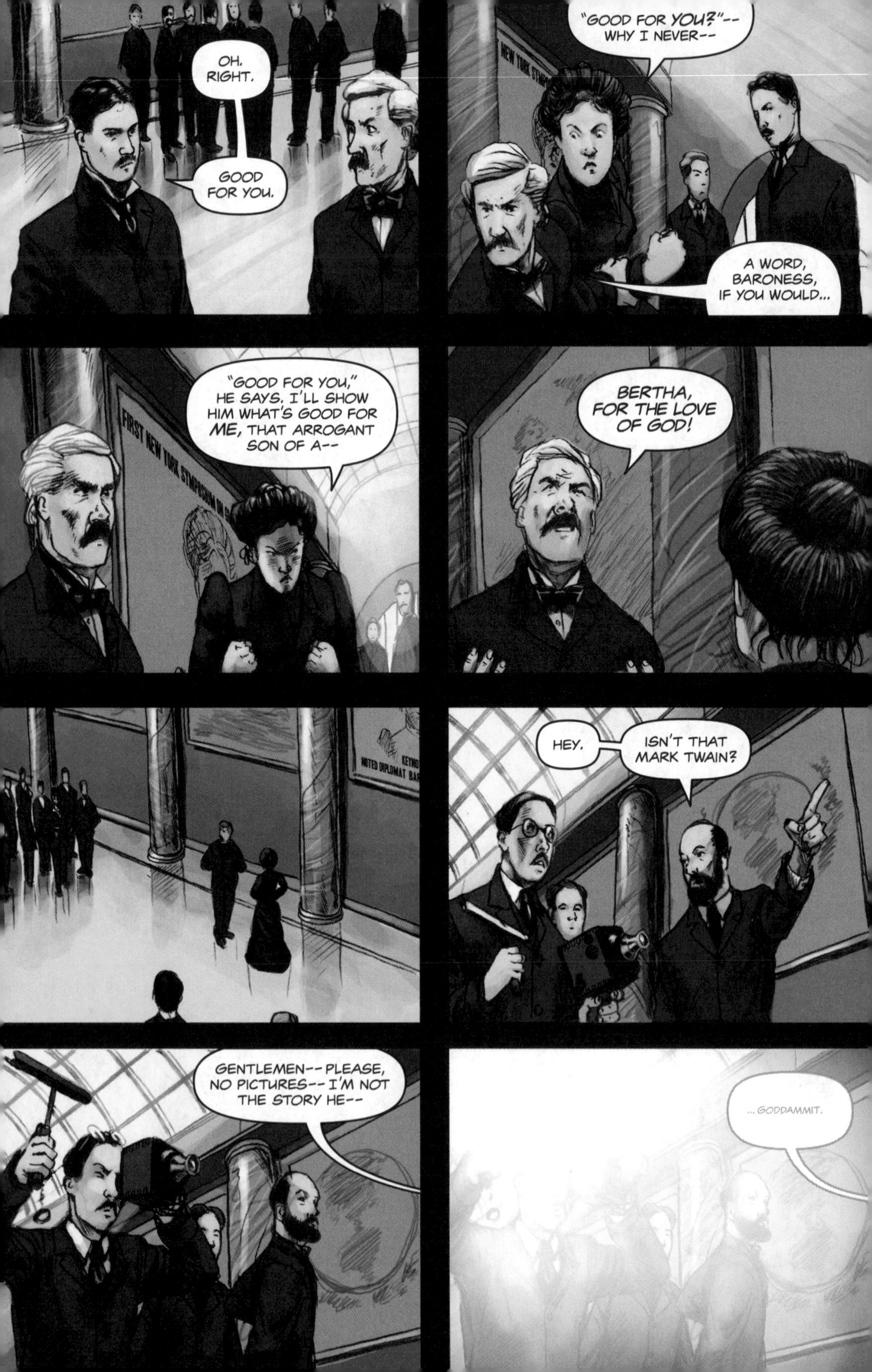
OH. RIGHT.
GOOD FOR YOU.
"GOOD FOR YOU?"-- WHY I NEVER--
A WORD, BARONESS, IF YOU WOULD...
"GOOD FOR YOU," HE SAYS. I'LL SHOW HIM WHAT'S GOOD FOR ME, THAT ARROGANT SON OF A--
BERTHA, FOR THE LOVE OF GOD!
HEY.
ISN'T THAT MARK TWAIN?
GENTLEMEN-- PLEASE, NO PICTURES-- I'M NOT THE STORY HE--
...GODDAMMIT.

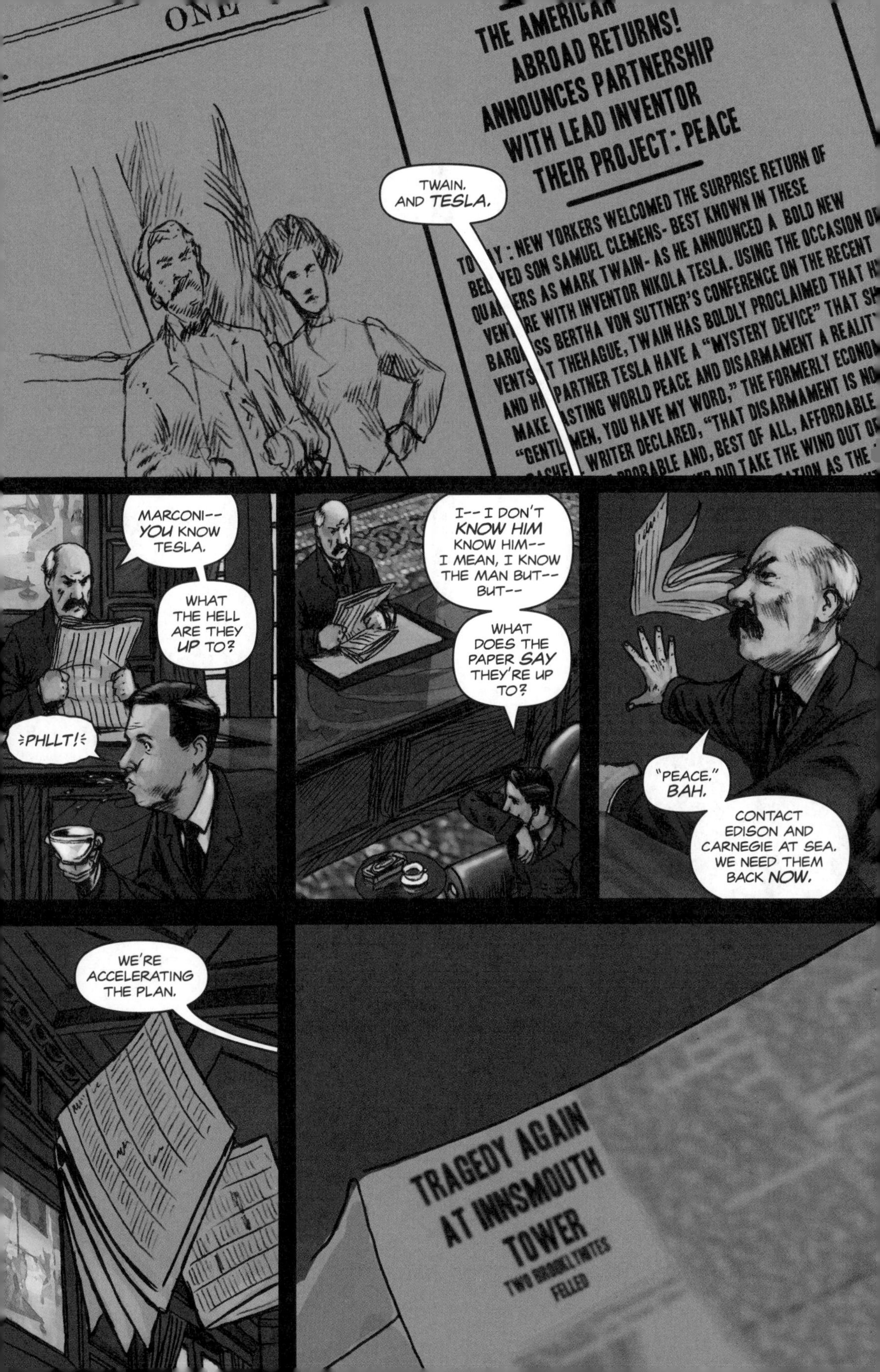
ONE
THE AMERICAN ABROAD RETURNS! ANNOUNCES PARTNERSHIP WITH LEAD INVENTOR THEIR PROJECT: PEACE
TWAIN. AND TESLA.
MARCONI-- YOU KNOW TESLA.
WHAT THE HELL ARE THEY UP TO?
PHLLT!
I-- I DON'T KNOW HIM KNOW HIM-- I MEAN, I KNOW THE MAN BUT-- BUT--
WHAT DOES THE PAPER SAY THEY'RE UP TO?
"PEACE." BAH.
CONTACT EDISON AND CARNEGIE AT SEA. WE NEED THEM BACK NOW.
WE'RE ACCELERATING THE PLAN.
TRAGEDY AGAIN AT INNSMOUTH TOWER

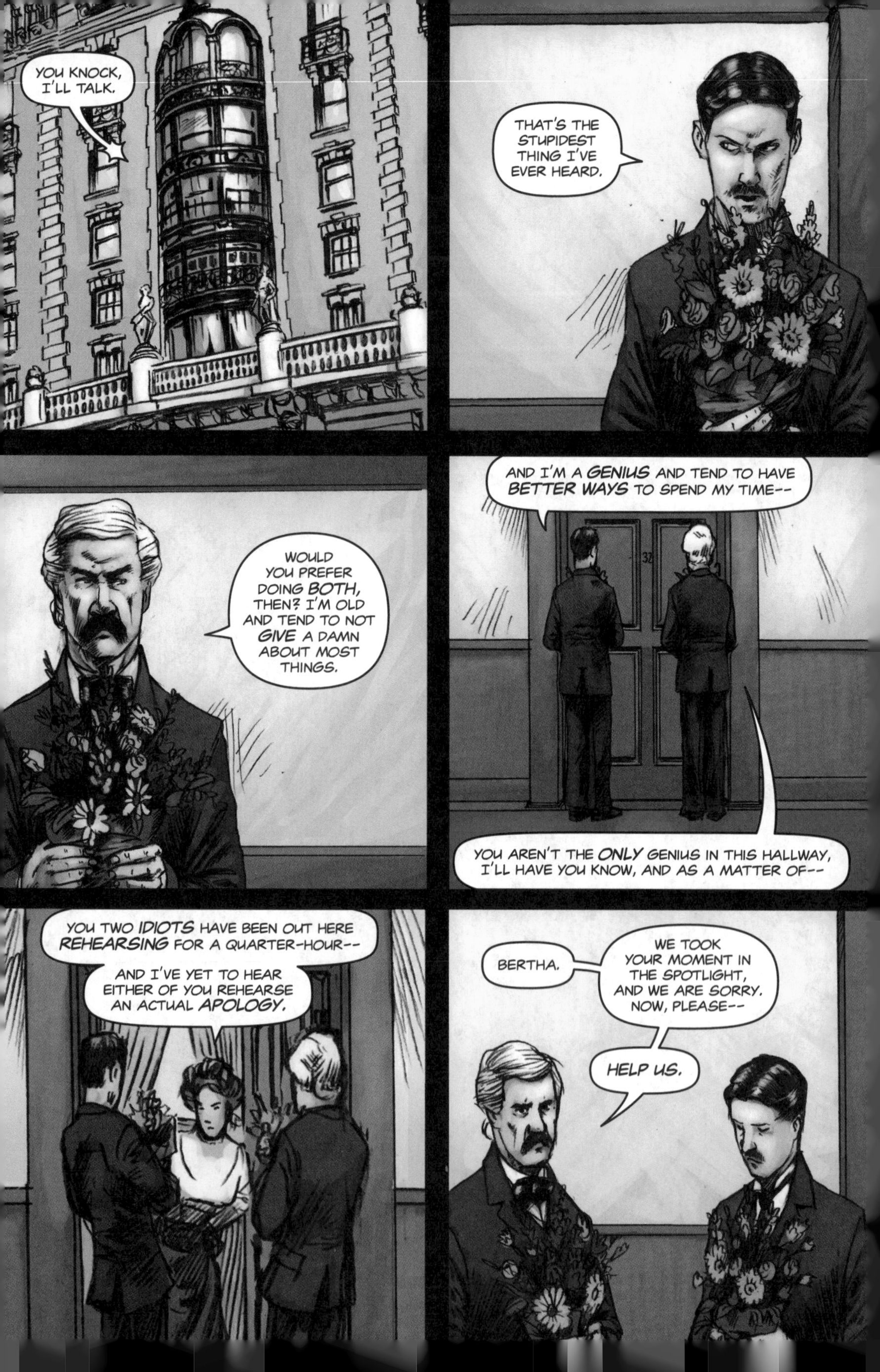
YOU KNOCK, I'LL TALK.
THAT'S THE STUPIDEST THING I'VE EVER HEARD.
WOULD YOU PREFER DOING BOTH, THEN? I'M OLD AND TEND TO NOT GIVE A DAMN ABOUT MOST THINGS.
AND I'M A GENIUS AND TEND TO HAVE BETTER WAYS TO SPEND MY TIME--
YOU AREN'T THE ONLY GENIUS IN THIS HALLWAY, I'LL HAVE YOU KNOW, AND AS A MATTER OF--
YOU TWO IDIOTS HAVE BEEN OUT HERE REHEARSING FOR A QUARTER-HOUR--
AND I'VE YET TO HEAR EITHER OF YOU REHEARSE AN ACTUAL APOLOGY.
BERTHA.
WE TOOK YOUR MOMENT IN THE SPOTLIGHT, AND WE ARE SORRY. NOW, PLEASE--
HELP US.

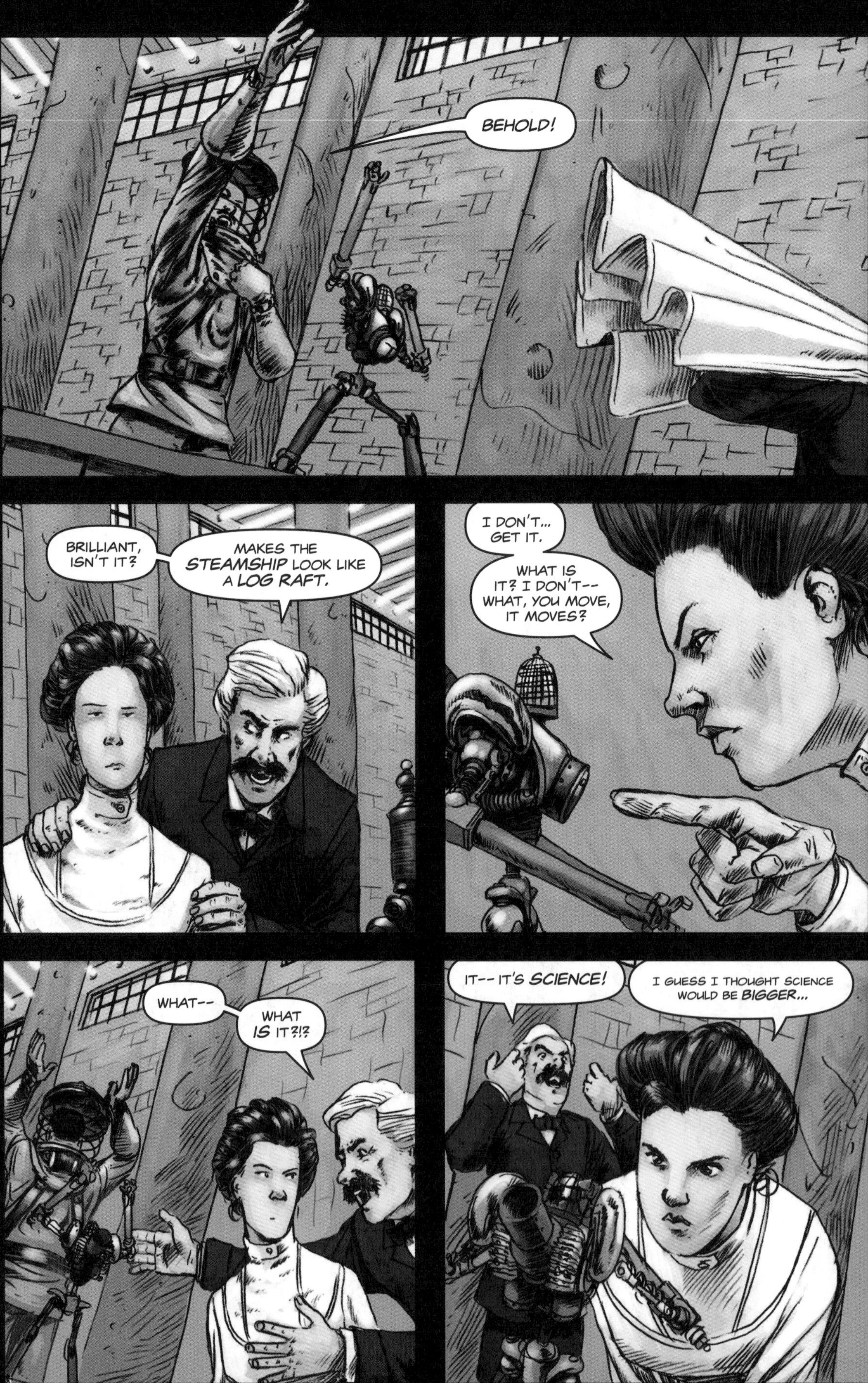
BEHOLD!
BRILLIANT, ISN'T IT?
MAKES THE STEAMSHIP LOOK LIKE A LOG RAFT.
I DON'T... GET IT.
WHAT IS IT? I DON'T-- WHAT, YOU MOVE, IT MOVES?
WHAT--
WHAT IS IT?!?
IT-- IT'S SCIENCE!
I GUESS I THOUGHT SCIENCE WOULD BE BIGGER...

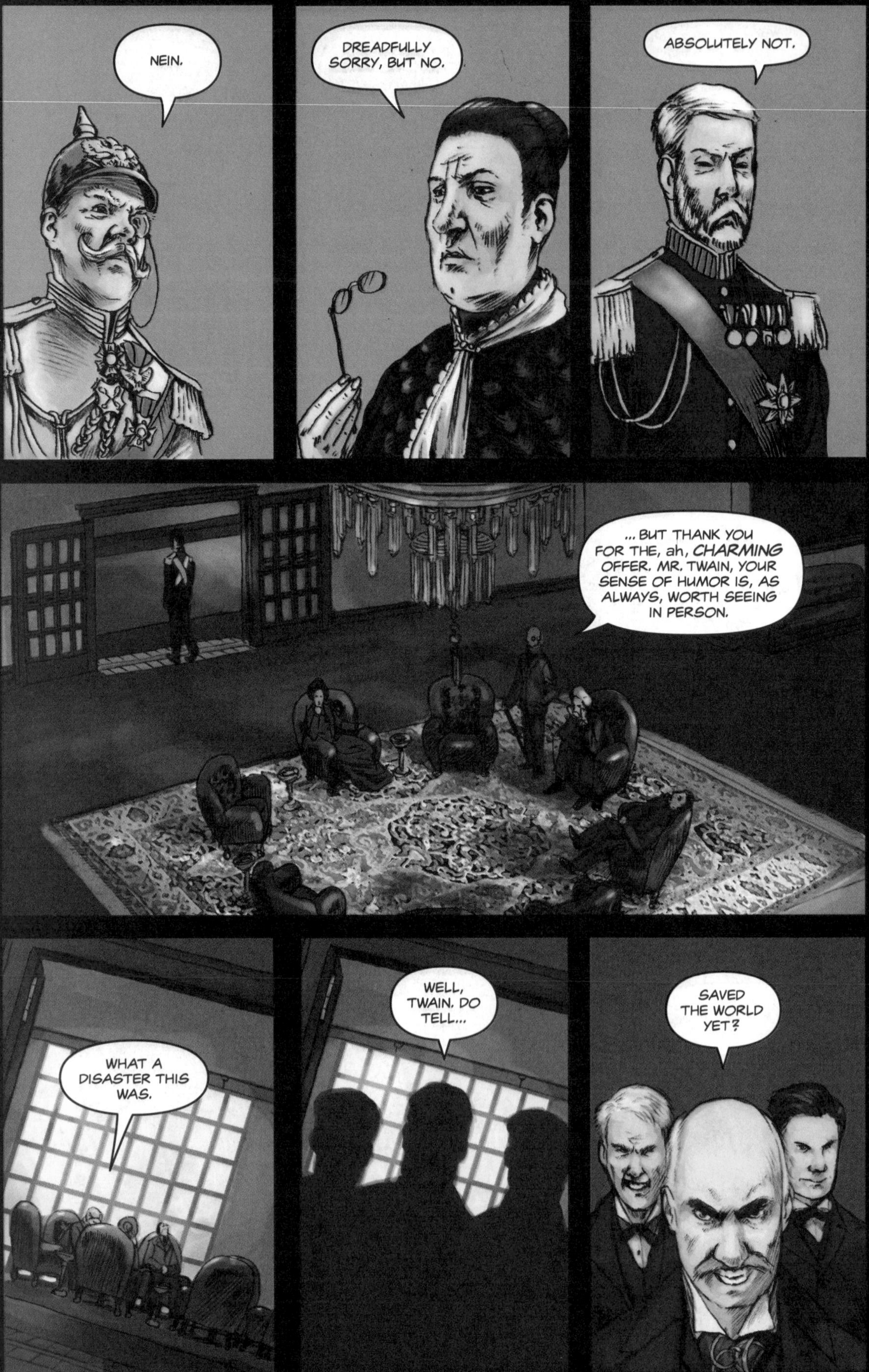
NEIN.
DREADFULLY SORRY, BUT NO.
ABSOLUTELY NOT.
... BUT THANK YOU FOR THE, ah, CHARMING OFFER. MR. TWAIN, YOUR SENSE OF HUMOR IS, AS ALWAYS, WORTH SEEING IN PERSON.
WHAT A DISASTER THIS WAS.
WELL, TWAIN. DO TELL...
SAVED THE WORLD YET?

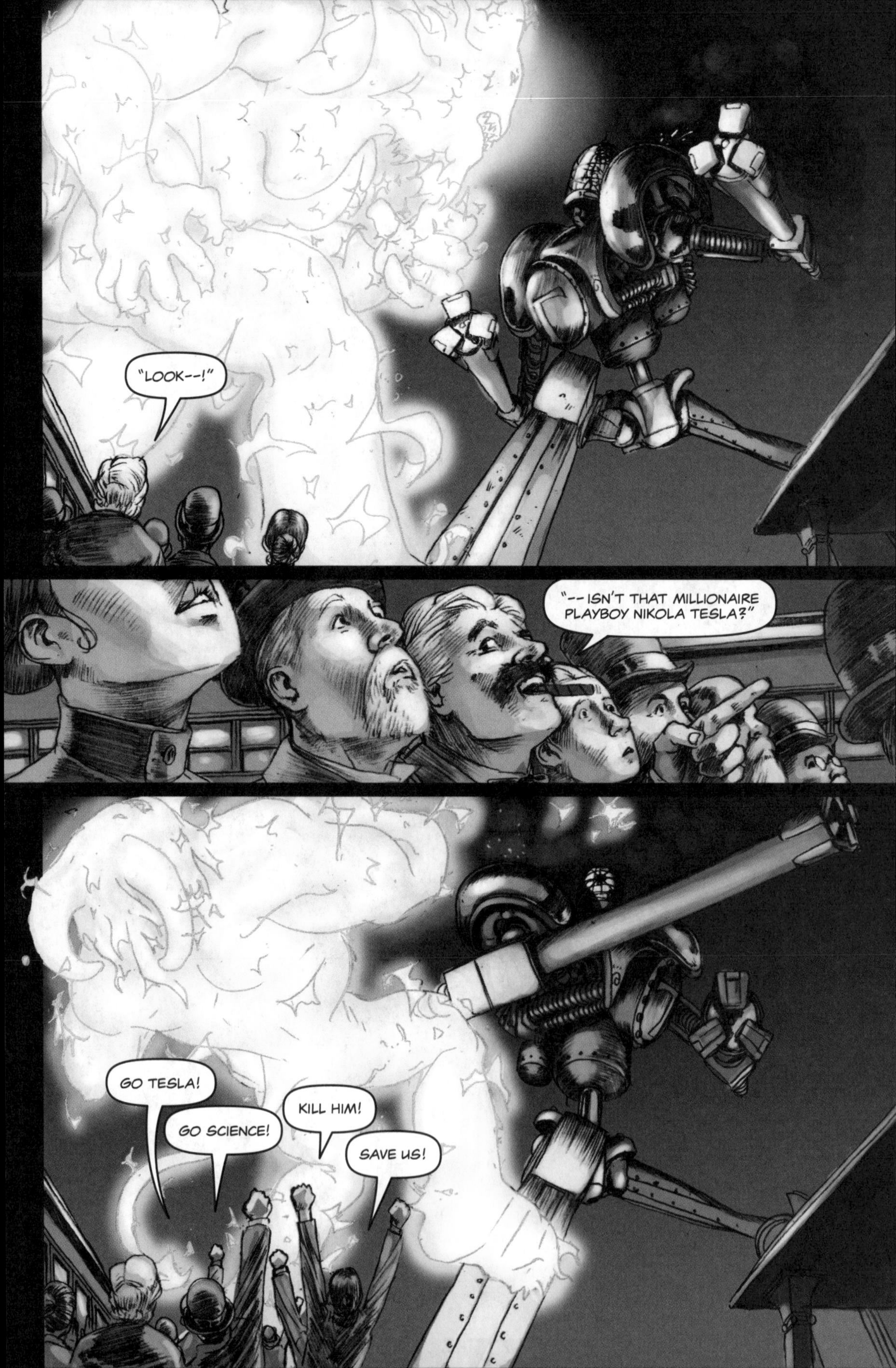
"LOOK--!"
"--ISN'T THAT MILLIONAIRE PLAYBOY NIKOLA TESLA?"
GO TESLA!
GO SCIENCE!
KILL HIM!
SAVE US!

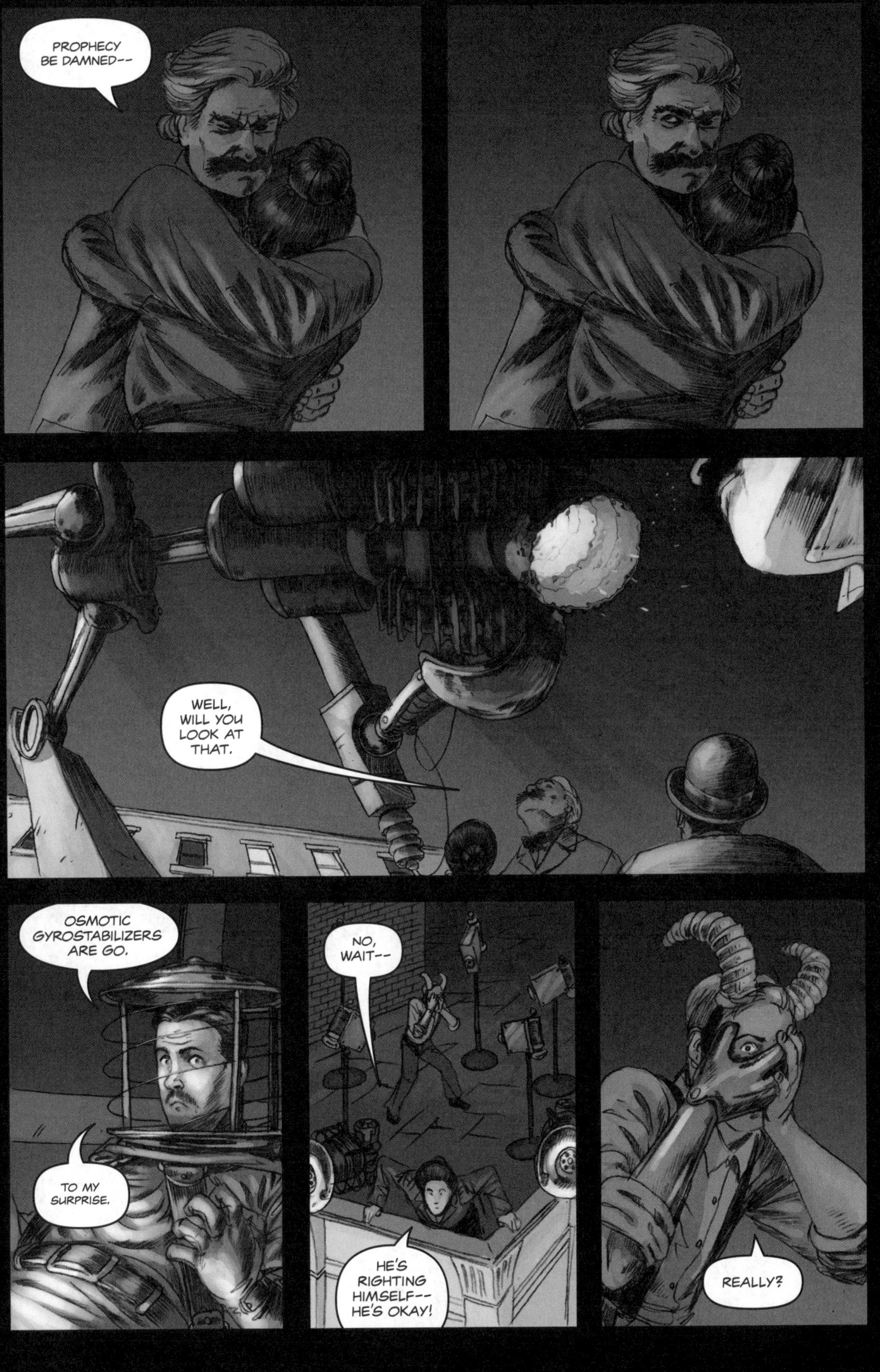
PROPHECY BE DAMNED--
WELL, WILL YOU LOOK AT THAT.
OSMOTIC GYROSTABILIZERS ARE GO.
TO MY SURPRISE.
NO, WAIT--
HE'S RIGHTING HIMSELF-- HE'S OKAY!
REALLY?

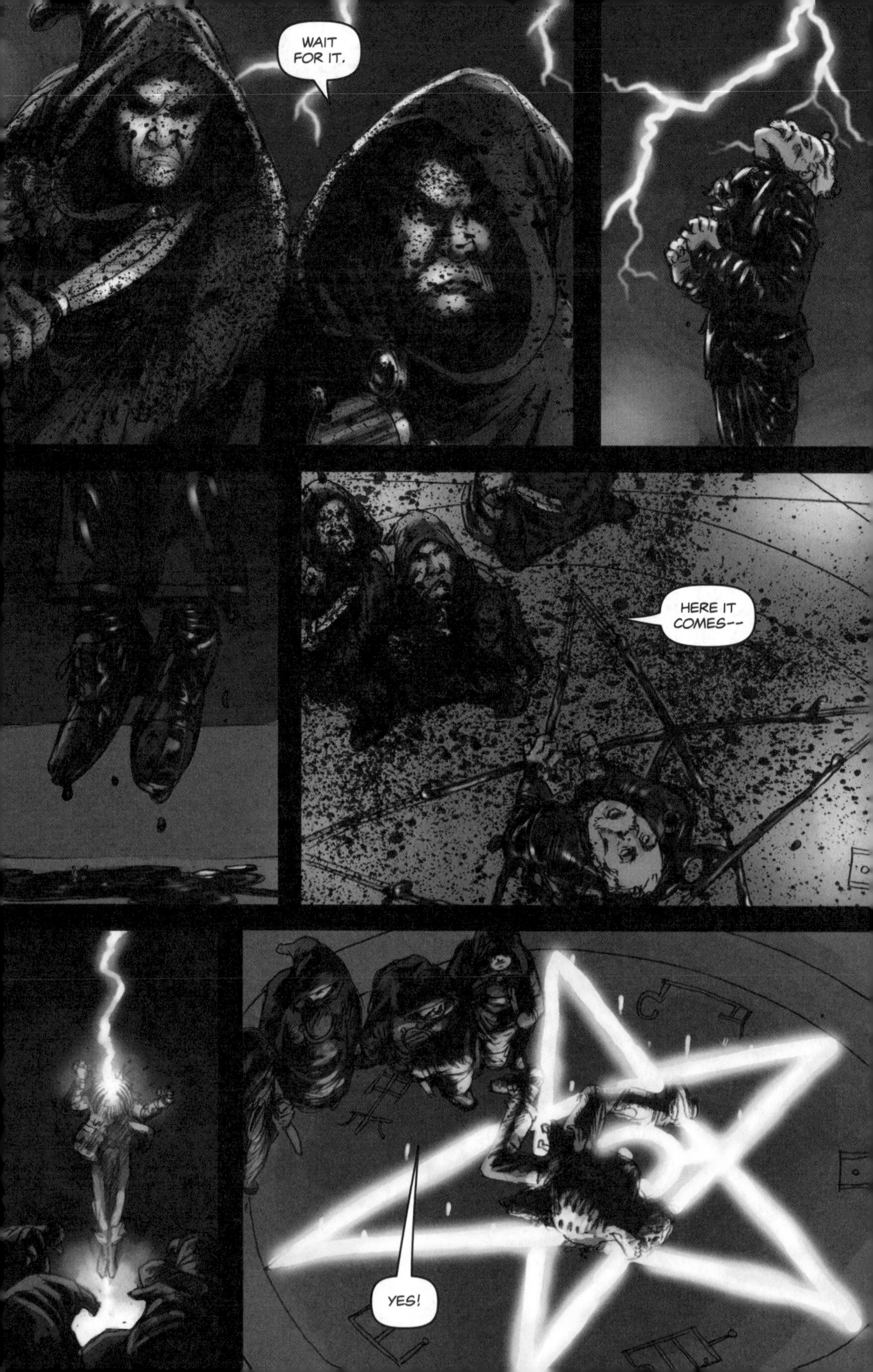
WAIT FOR IT.
HERE IT COMES--
YES!

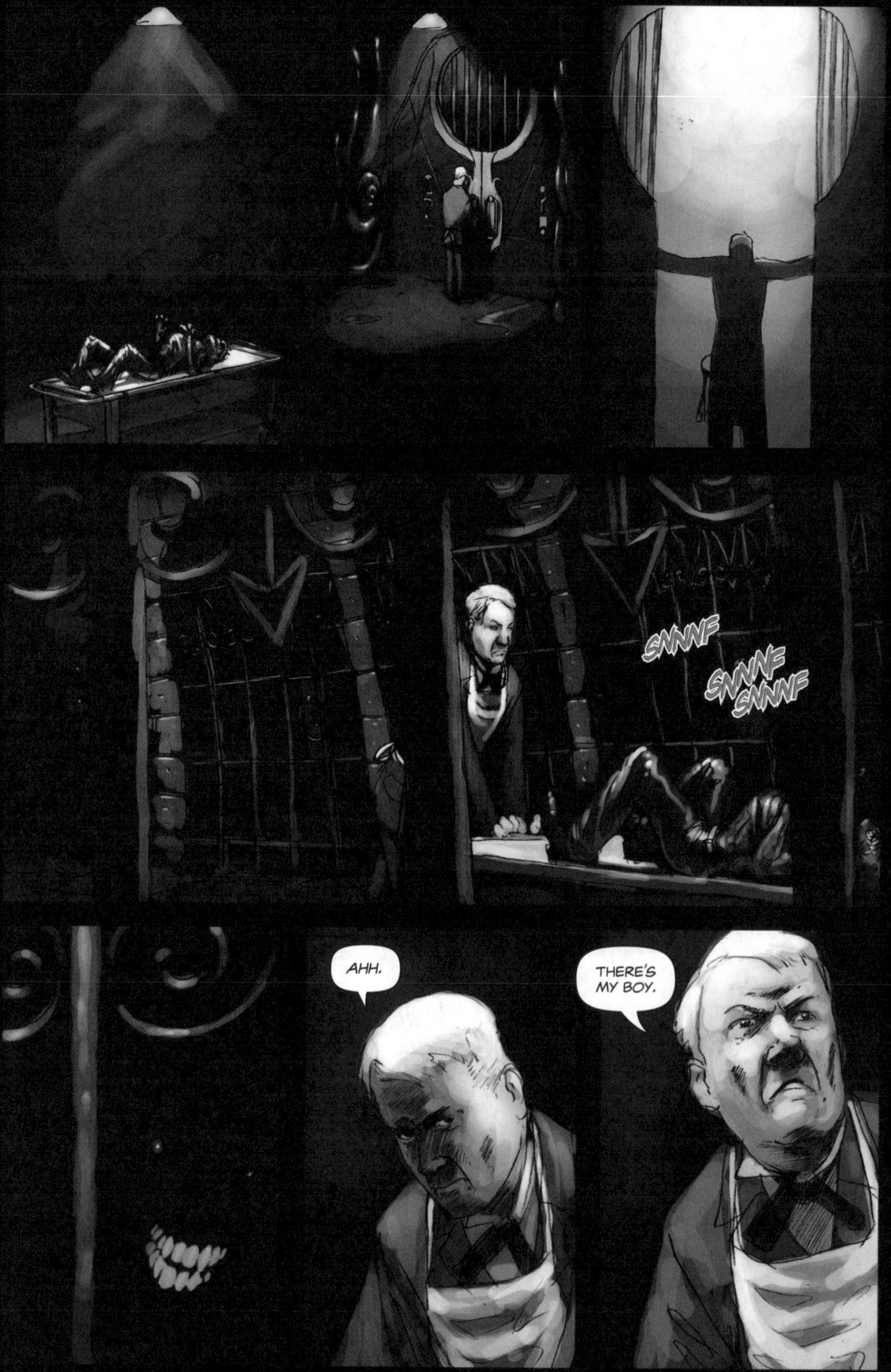
SNNNF
SNNNF
SNNNF
AHH.
THERE'S MY BOY.

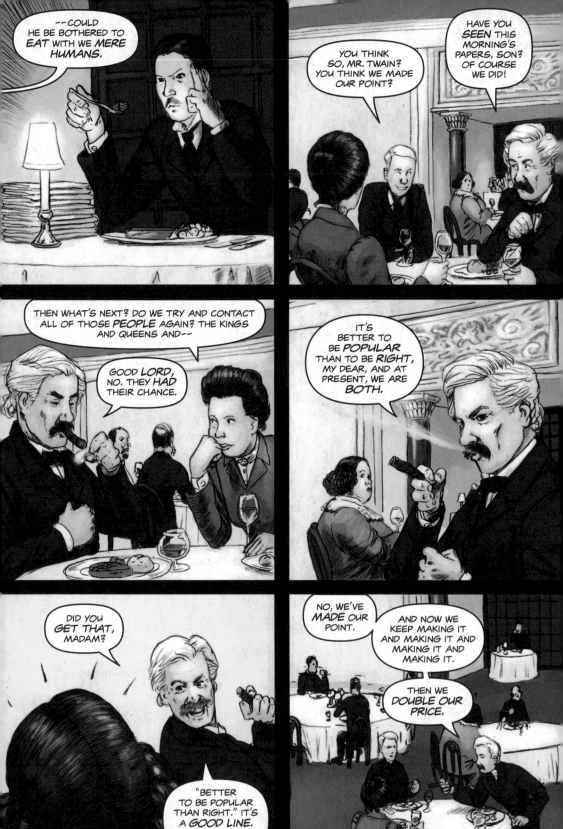

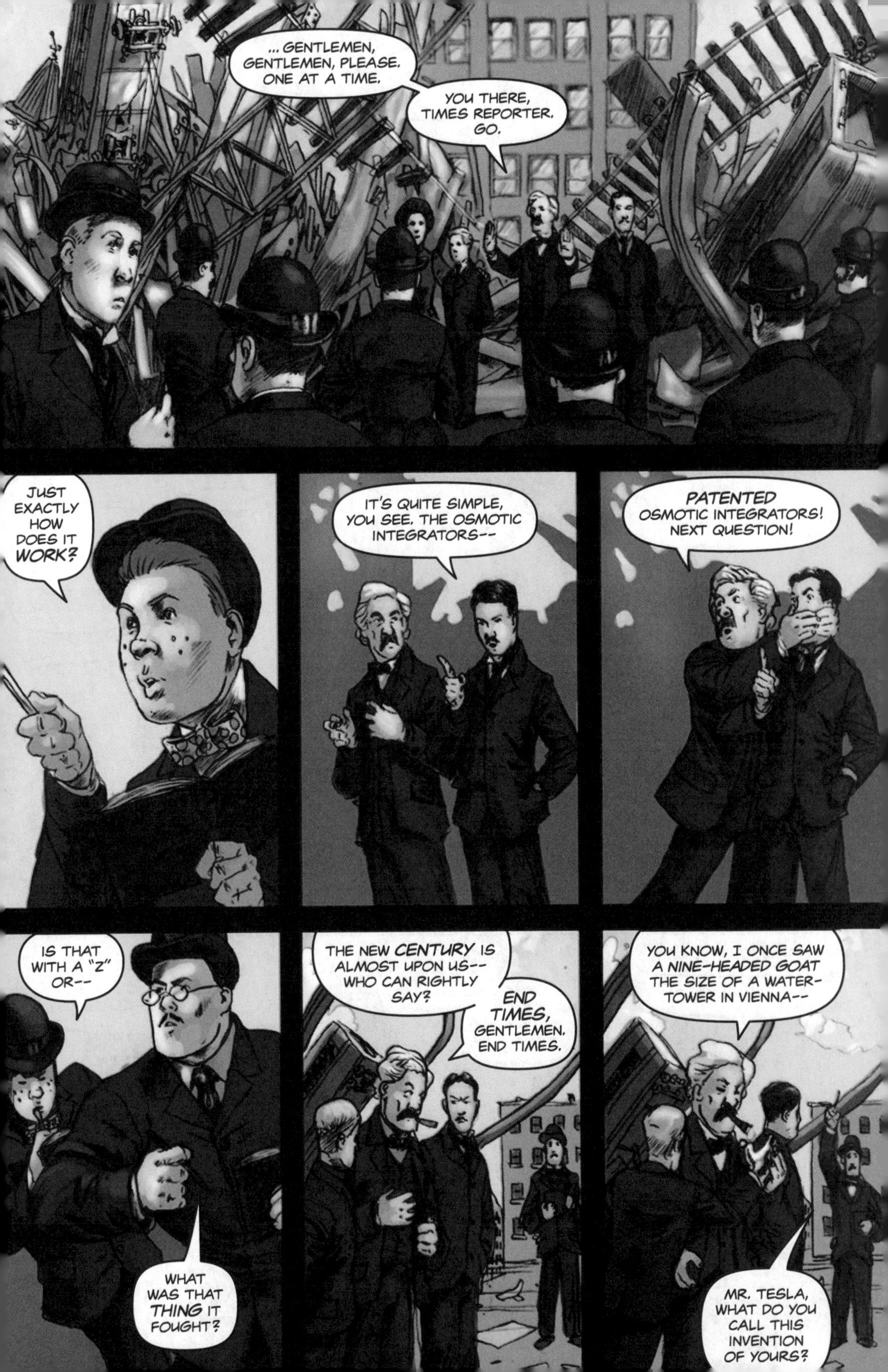
... GENTLEMEN, GENTLEMEN, PLEASE. ONE AT A TIME.
YOU THERE, TIMES REPORTER. GO.
JUST EXACTLY HOW DOES IT WORK?
IT'S QUITE SIMPLE, YOU SEE. THE OSMOTIC INTEGRATORS--
PATENTED OSMOTIC INTEGRATORS! NEXT QUESTION!
IS THAT WITH A "Z" OR--
WHAT WAS THAT THING IT FOUGHT?
THE NEW CENTURY IS ALMOST UPON US-- WHO CAN RIGHTLY SAY?
END TIMES, GENTLEMEN. END TIMES.
YOU KNOW, I ONCE SAW A NINE-HEADED GOAT THE SIZE OF A WATER-TOWER IN VIENNA--
MR. TESLA, WHAT DO YOU CALL THIS INVENTION OF YOURS?

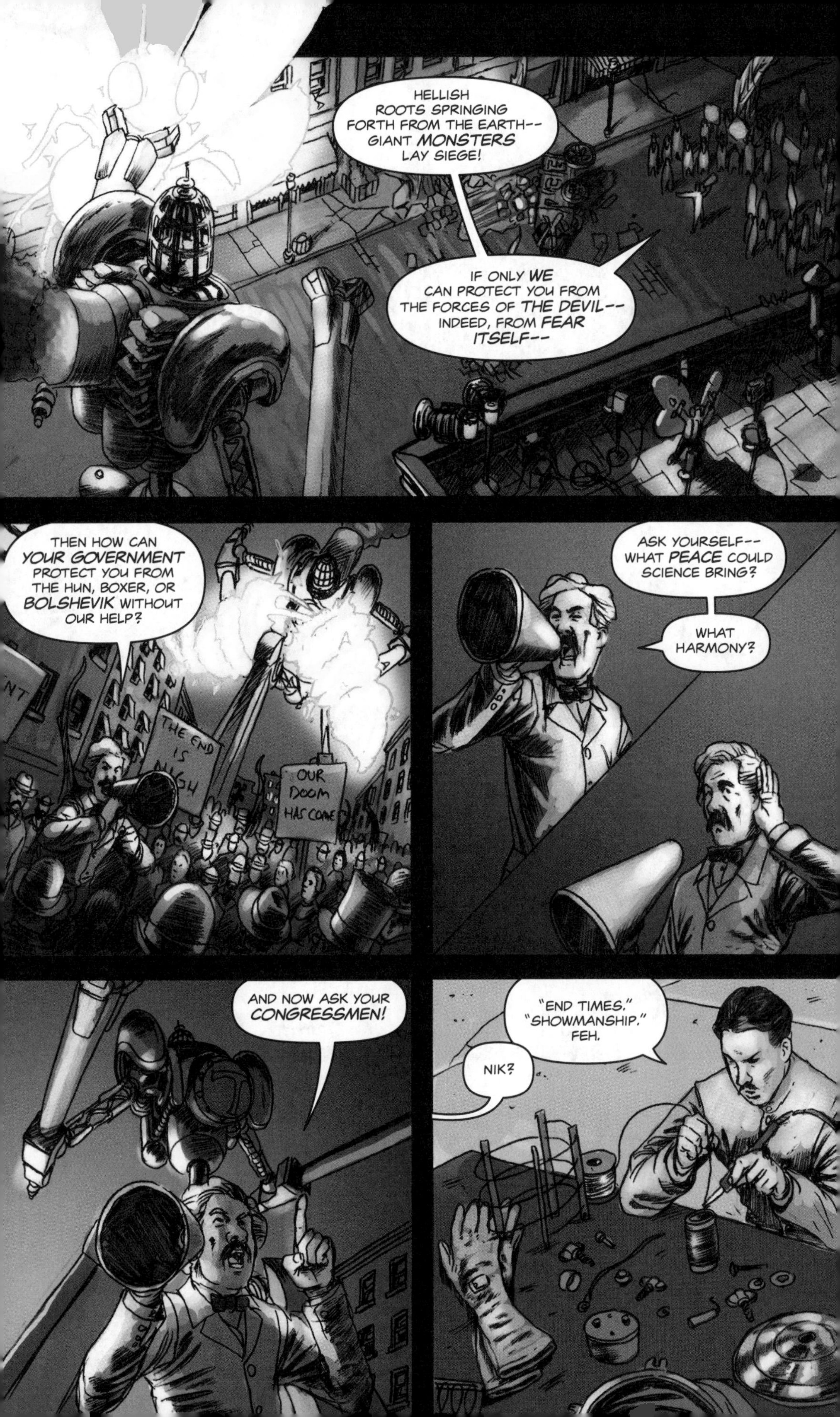
HELLISH ROOTS SPRINGING FORTH FROM THE EARTH-- GIANT MONSTERS LAY SIEGE!
IF ONLY WE CAN PROTECT YOU FROM THE FORCES OF THE DEVIL-- INDEED, FROM FEAR ITSELF--
THEN HOW CAN YOUR GOVERNMENT PROTECT YOU FROM THE HUN, BOXER, OR BOLSHEVIK WITHOUT OUR HELP?
THE END IS NIGH
OUR DOOM HAS COME
ASK YOURSELF-- WHAT PEACE COULD SCIENCE BRING?
WHAT HARMONY?
AND NOW ASK YOUR CONGRESSMEN!
"END TIMES." "SHOWMANSHIP." FEH.
NIK?

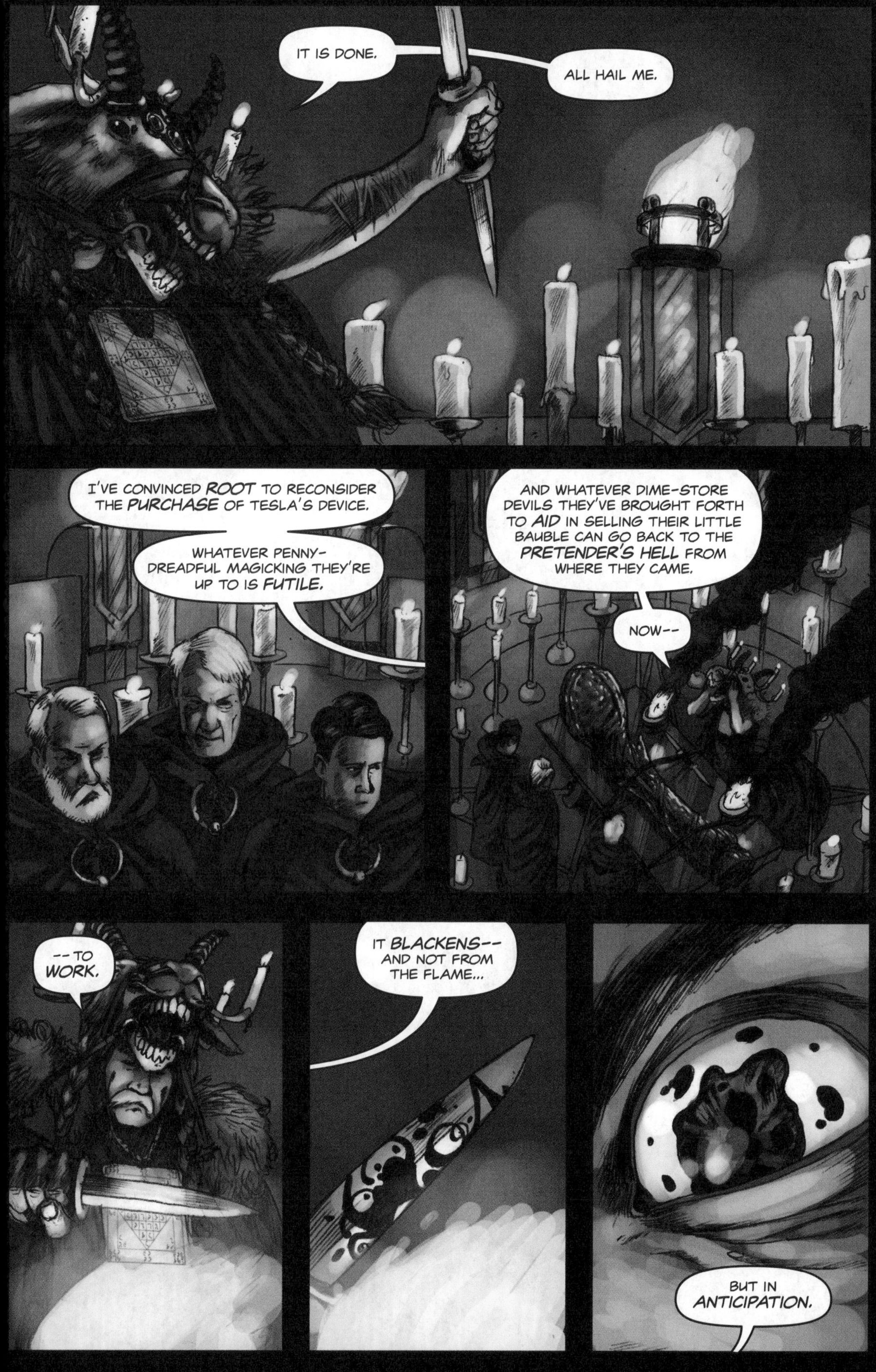
IT IS DONE.
ALL HAIL ME.
I'VE CONVINCED ROOT TO RECONSIDER THE PURCHASE OF TESLA'S DEVICE.
WHATEVER PENNY-DREADFUL MAGICKING THEY'RE UP TO IS FUTILE.
AND WHATEVER DIME-STORE DEVILS THEY'VE BROUGHT FORTH TO AID IN SELLING THEIR LITTLE BAUBLE CAN GO BACK TO THE PRETENDER'S HELL FROM WHERE THEY CAME.
NOW--
--TO WORK.
IT BLACKENS-- AND NOT FROM THE FLAME...
BUT IN ANTICIPATION.

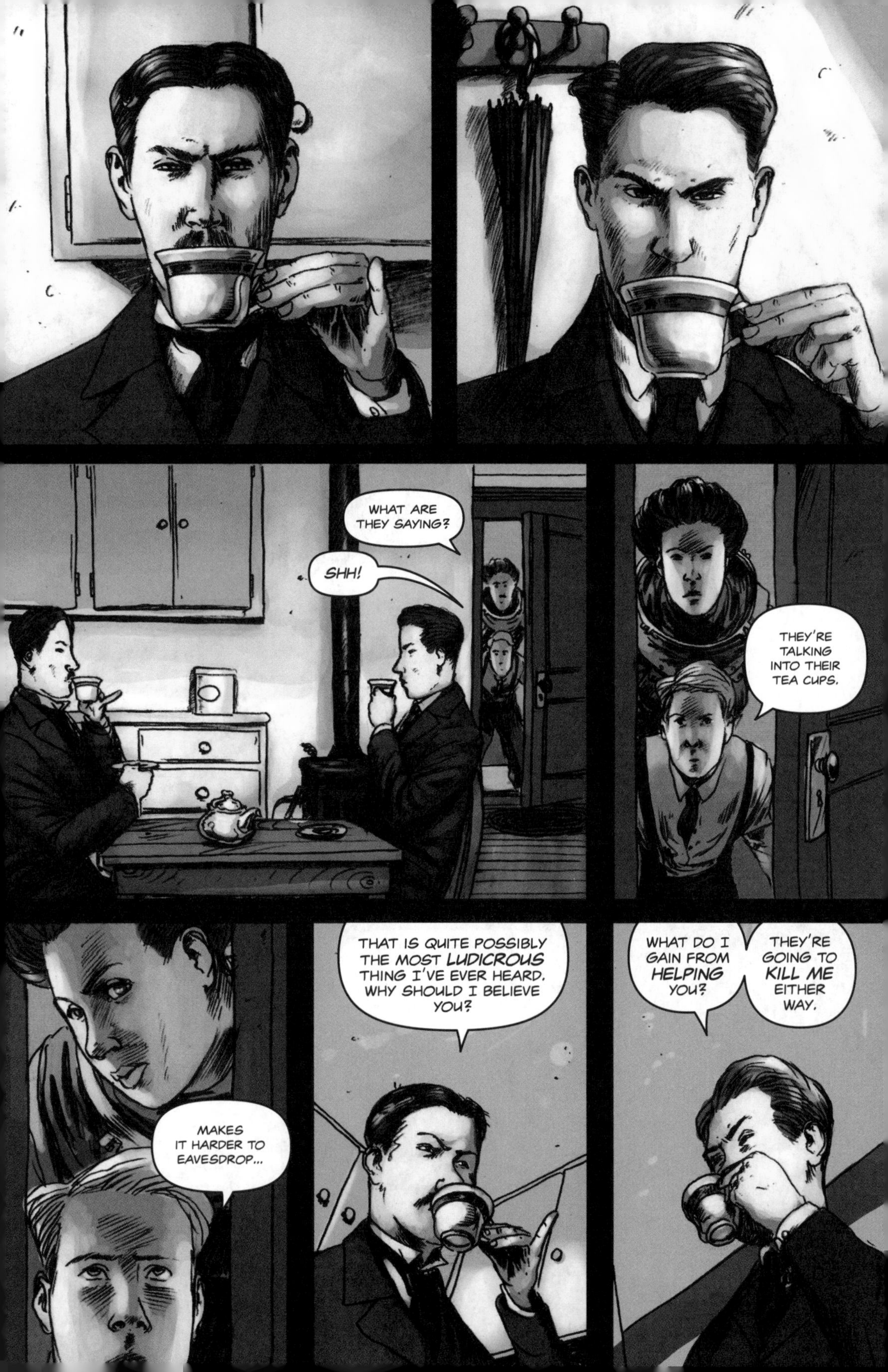
WHAT ARE THEY SAYING?
SHH!
THEY'RE TALKING INTO THEIR TEA CUPS.
MAKES IT HARDER TO EAVESDROP...
THAT IS QUITE POSSIBLY THE MOST LUDICROUS THING I'VE EVER HEARD. WHY SHOULD I BELIEVE YOU?
WHAT DO I GAIN FROM HELPING YOU?
THEY'RE GOING TO KILL ME EITHER WAY.

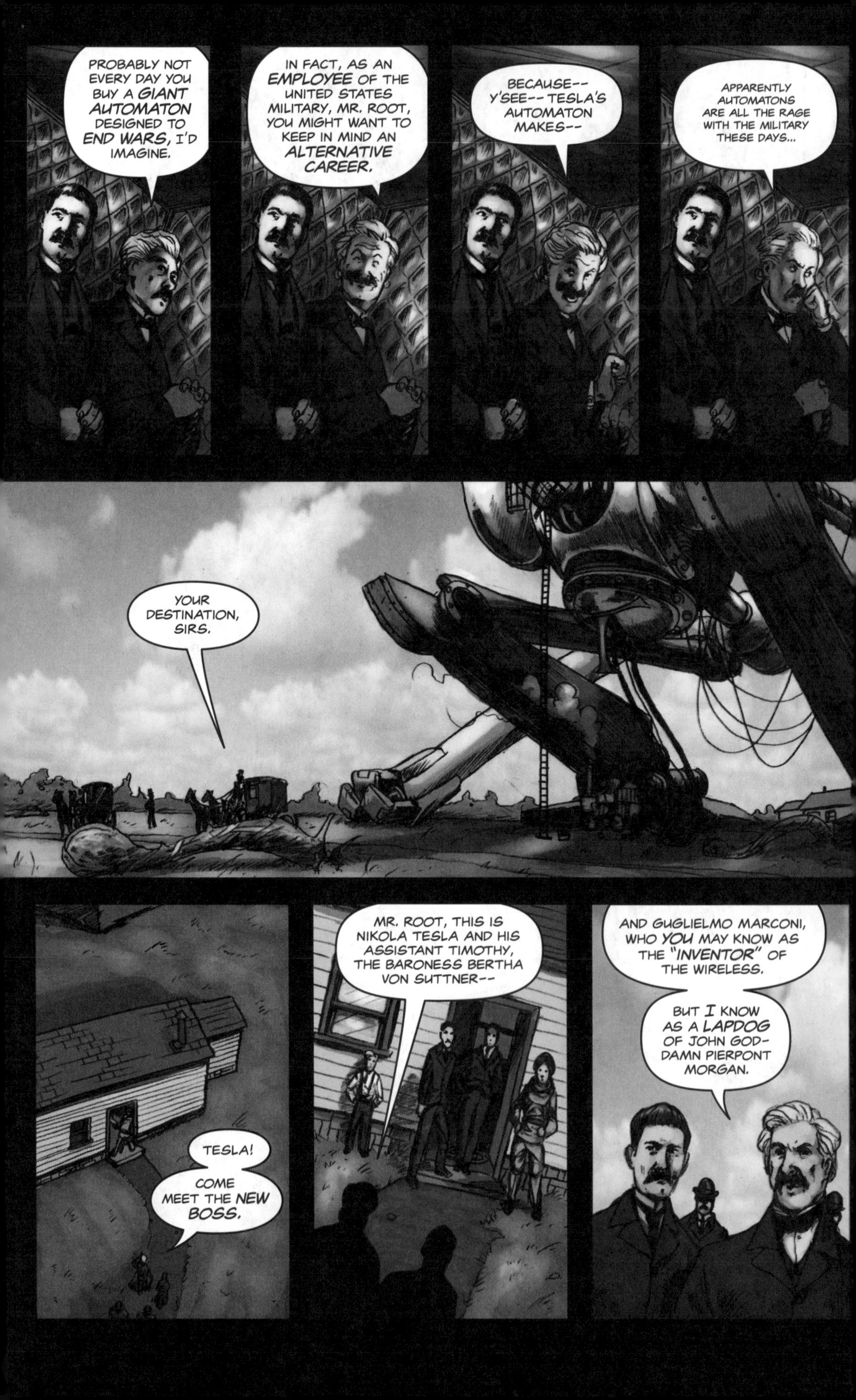
PROBABLY NOT EVERY DAY YOU BUY A GIANT AUTOMATON DESIGNED TO END WARS, I'D IMAGINE.
IN FACT, AS AN EMPLOYEE OF THE UNITED STATES MILITARY, MR. ROOT, YOU MIGHT WANT TO KEEP IN MIND AN ALTERNATIVE CAREER.
BECAUSE-- Y'SEE-- TESLA'S AUTOMATON MAKES--
APPARENTLY AUTOMATONS ARE ALL THE RAGE WITH THE MILITARY THESE DAYS...
YOUR DESTINATION, SIRS.
TESLA!
COME MEET THE NEW BOSS.
MR. ROOT, THIS IS NIKOLA TESLA AND HIS ASSISTANT TIMOTHY, THE BARONESS BERTHA VON SUTTNER--
AND GUGLIELMO MARCONI, WHO YOU MAY KNOW AS THE "INVENTOR" OF THE WIRELESS.
BUT I KNOW AS A LAPDOG OF JOHN GOD-DAMN PIERPONT MORGAN.

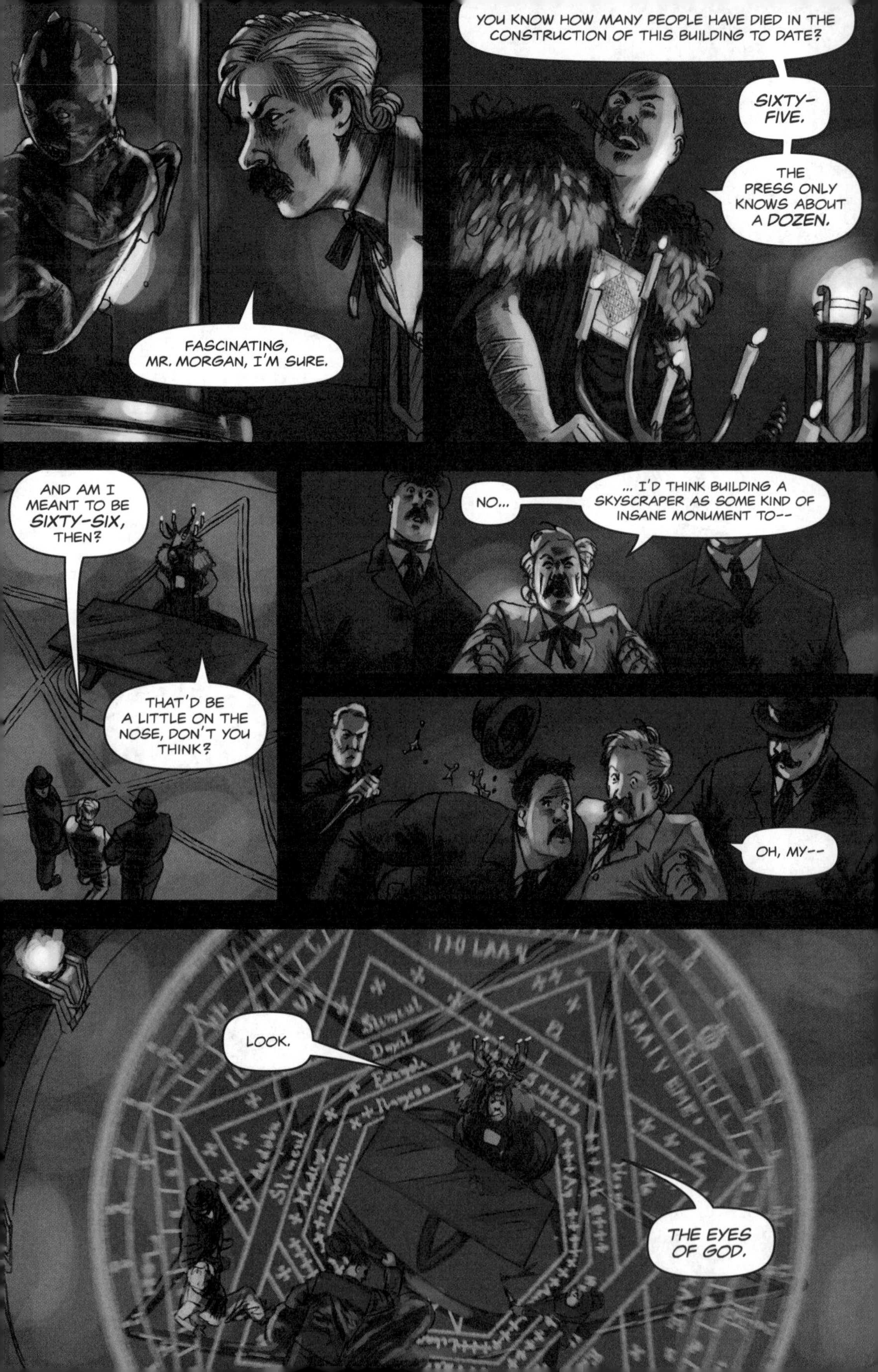
FASCINATING, MR. MORGAN, I'M SURE.
YOU KNOW HOW MANY PEOPLE HAVE DIED IN THE CONSTRUCTION OF THIS BUILDING TO DATE?
SIXTY-FIVE.
THE PRESS ONLY KNOWS ABOUT A DOZEN.
AND AM I MEANT TO BE SIXTY-SIX, THEN?
THAT'D BE A LITTLE ON THE NOSE, DON'T YOU THINK?
NO...
... I'D THINK BUILDING A SKYSCRAPER AS SOME KIND OF INSANE MONUMENT TO--
OH, MY--
LOOK.
THE EYES OF GOD.

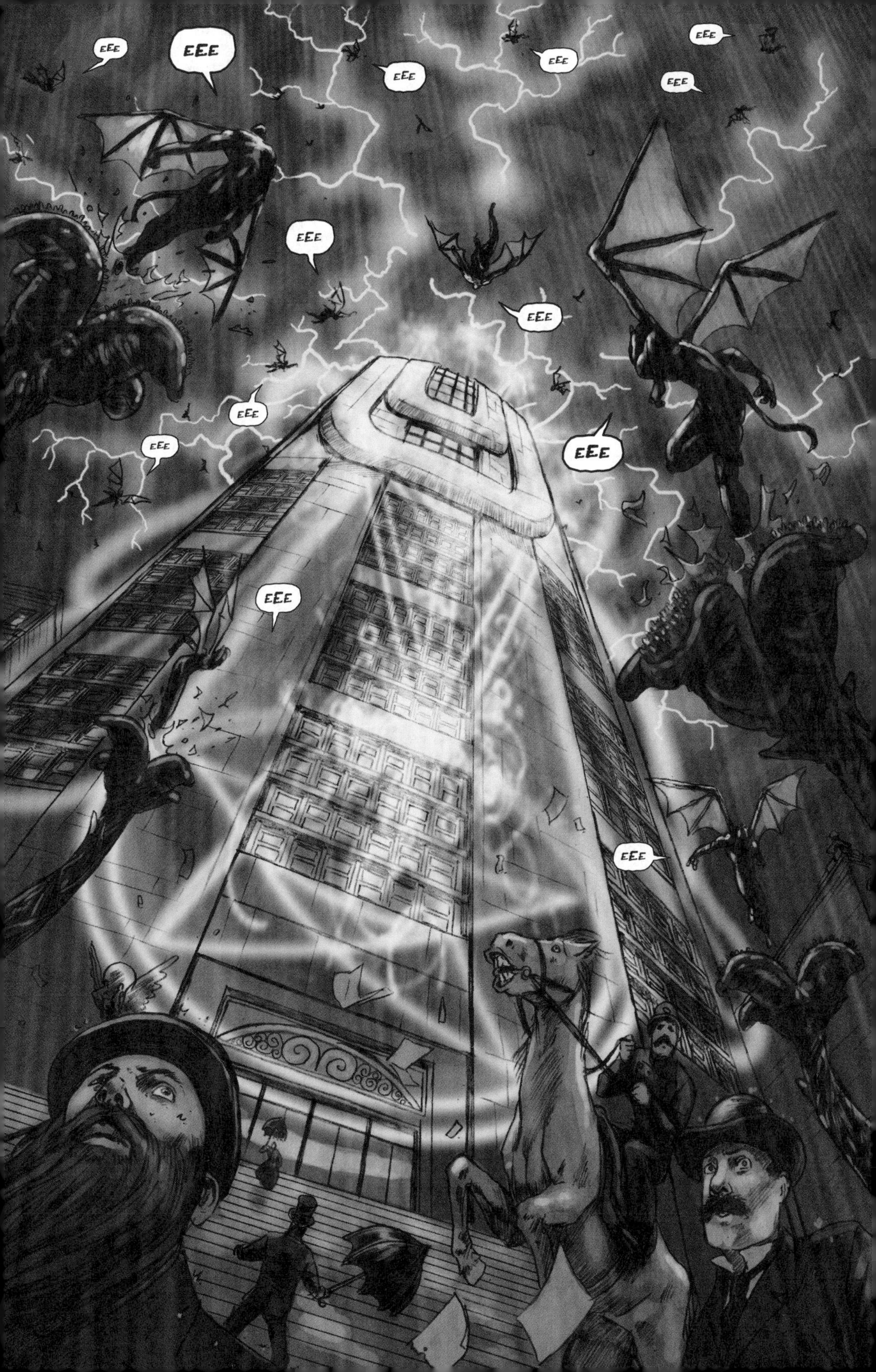
EEE
EEE
EEE
EEE
EEE
EEE
EEE
EEE
EEE
EEE
EEE
EEE
EEE

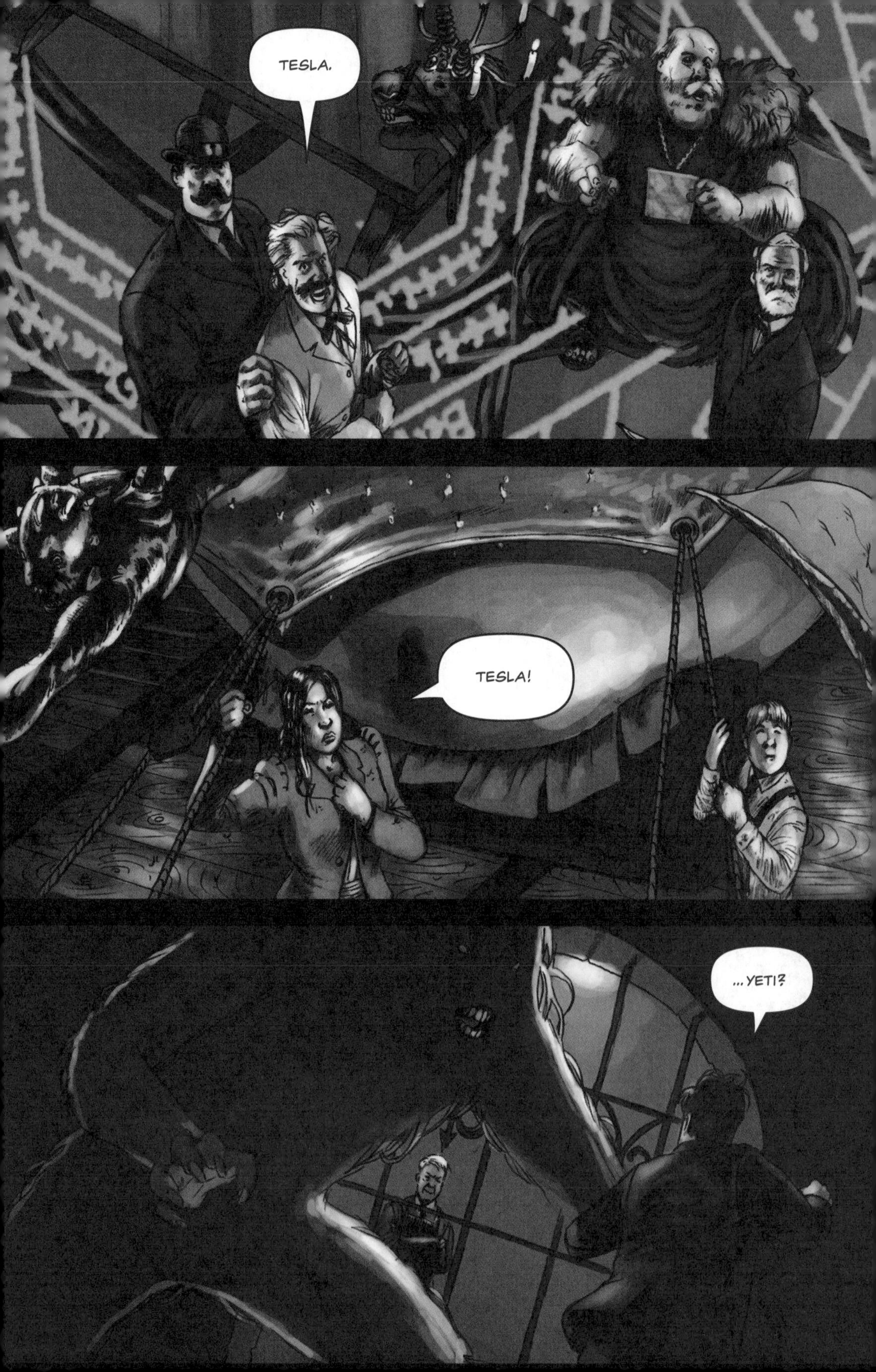
TESLA.
TESLA!
...YETI?

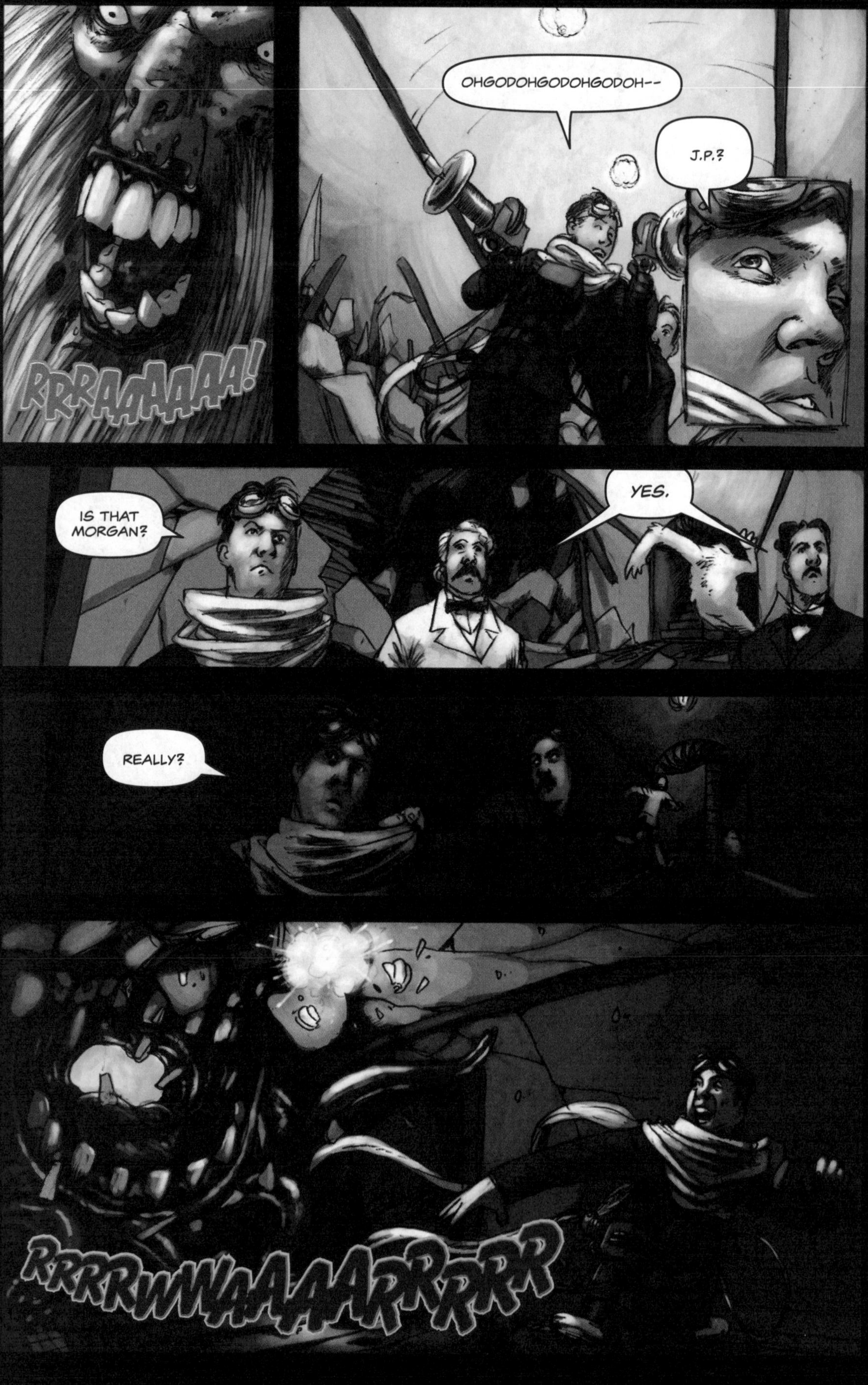
RRRAAAAAA!
OHGODOHGODOHGODOH--
J.P.?
IS THAT MORGAN?
YES.
REALLY?
RRRRWWAAAARRRRR

THE SUIT WAS NEVER *REALLY* THE WEAPON, SEE? IT WAS JUST THE *TRANSPORT.*

PROBLEM IS WE'VE ONLY GOT ONE SHOT AND IT'LL KILL OUR *POWER SUPPLY.*

MR. TESLA NEVER GOT IT OUT OF THE PROTOTYPE PHA--

ATTENTION TESLA MACHINE! TAKE DOWN THE BUILDING!

YOU CAN'T HURT LEVIATHAN! ONLY--

...AW, CRAP.

WHY'D HE STOP TALKING?

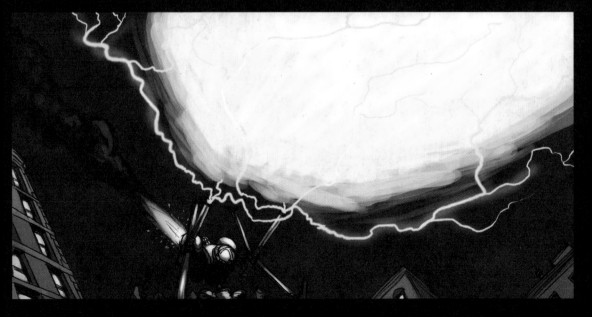

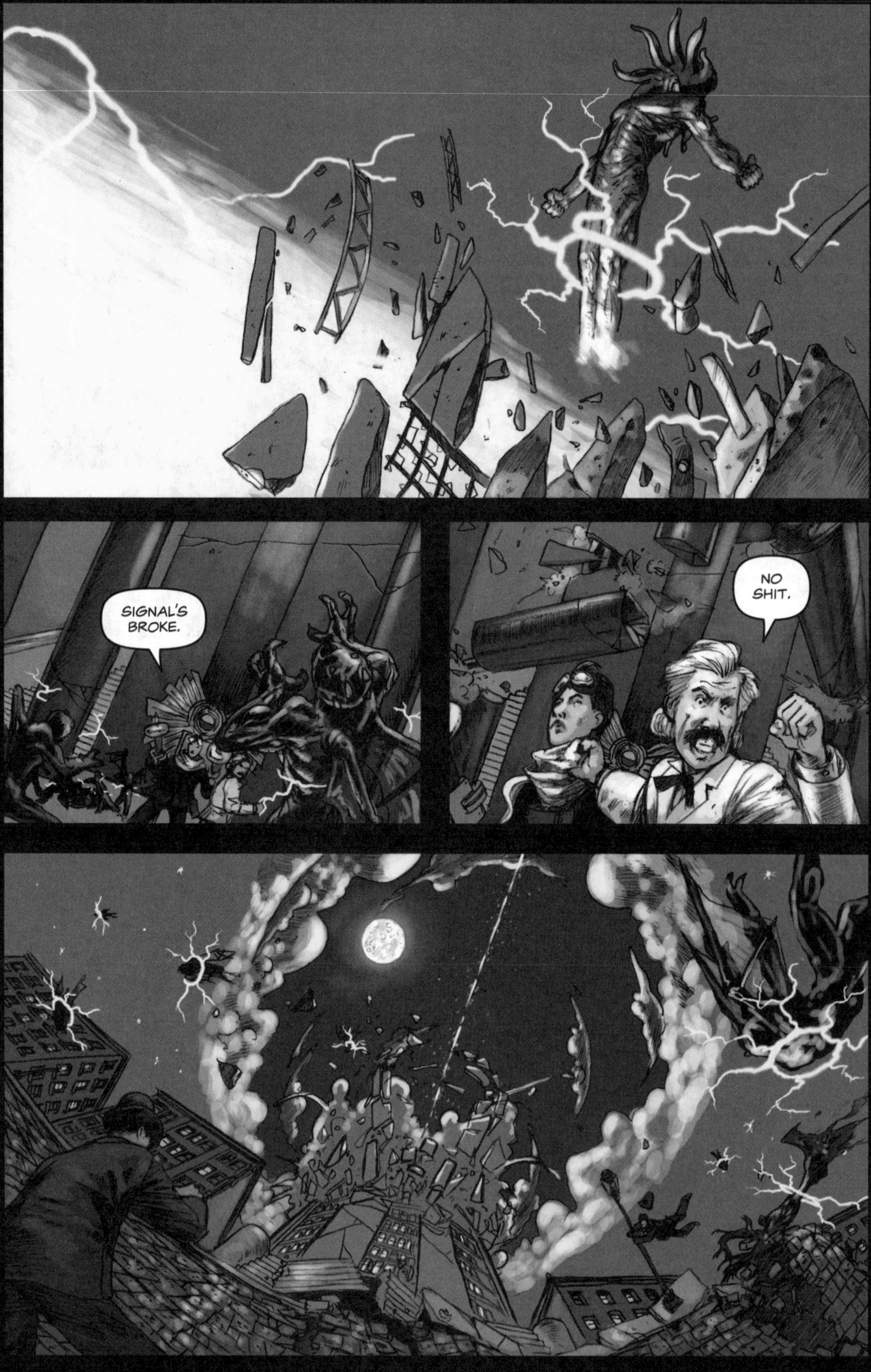
SIGNAL'S BROKE.
NO SHIT.

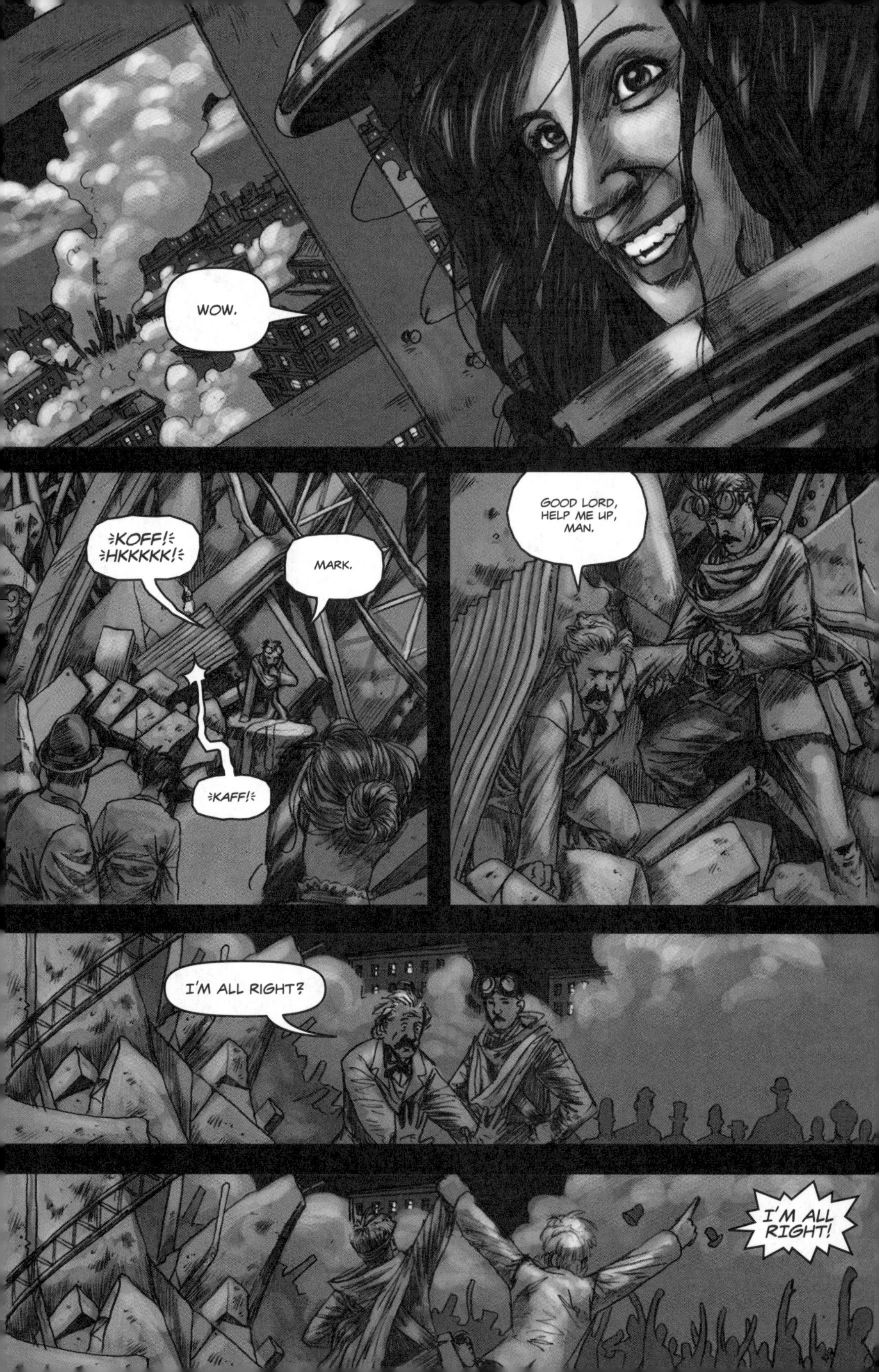
WOW.
KOFF! HKKKKK!
KAFF!
MARK.
GOOD LORD, HELP ME UP, MAN.
I'M ALL RIGHT?
I'M ALL RIGHT!

INQUIRIES

CONCERNING

CONCEPT ART

OF

SUNDRY ITEMS

EIGHTEENTH EDITION.

LONDON:

JOHN MURRAY, ALBEMARLE STREET.

1899.

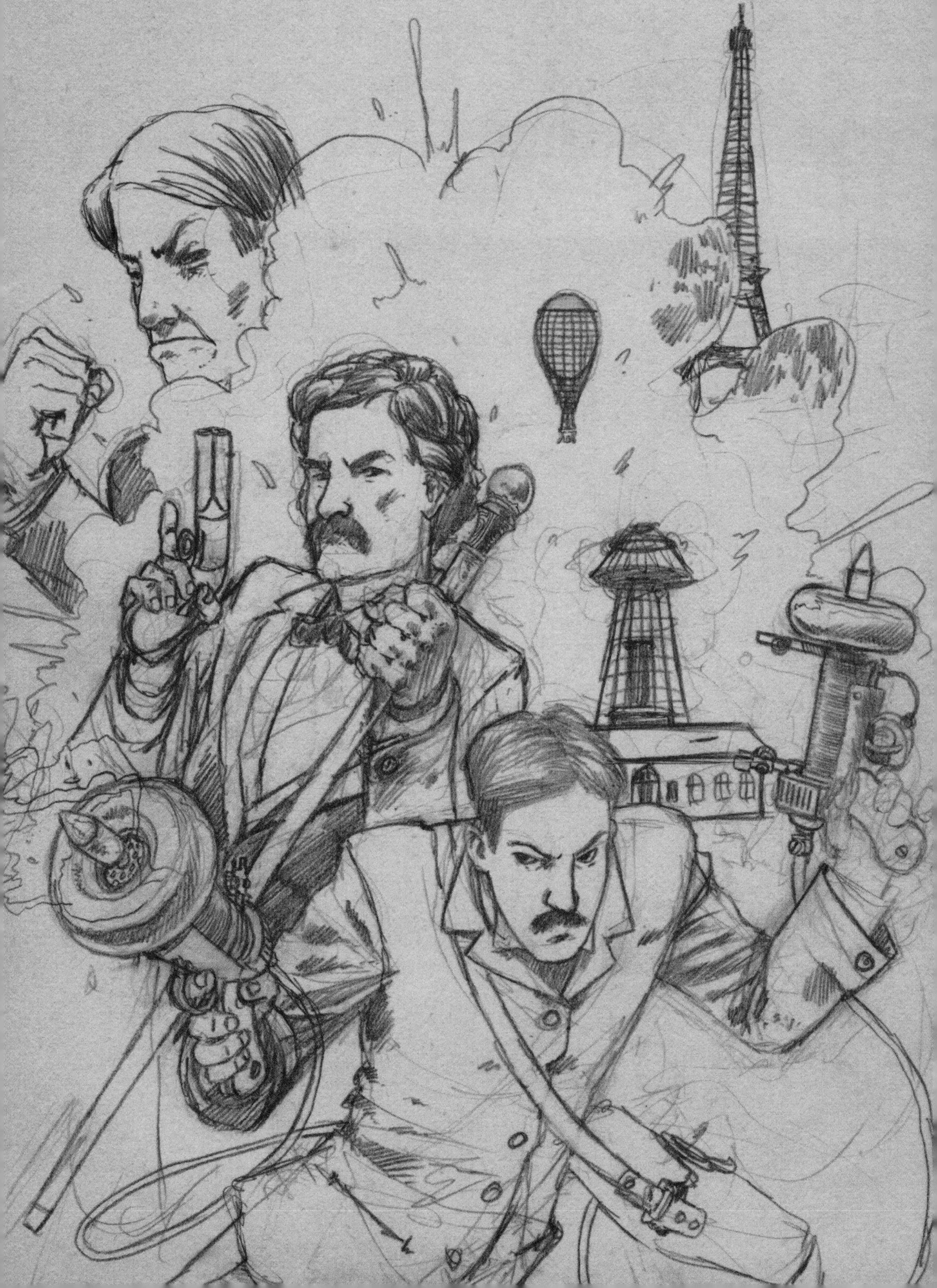

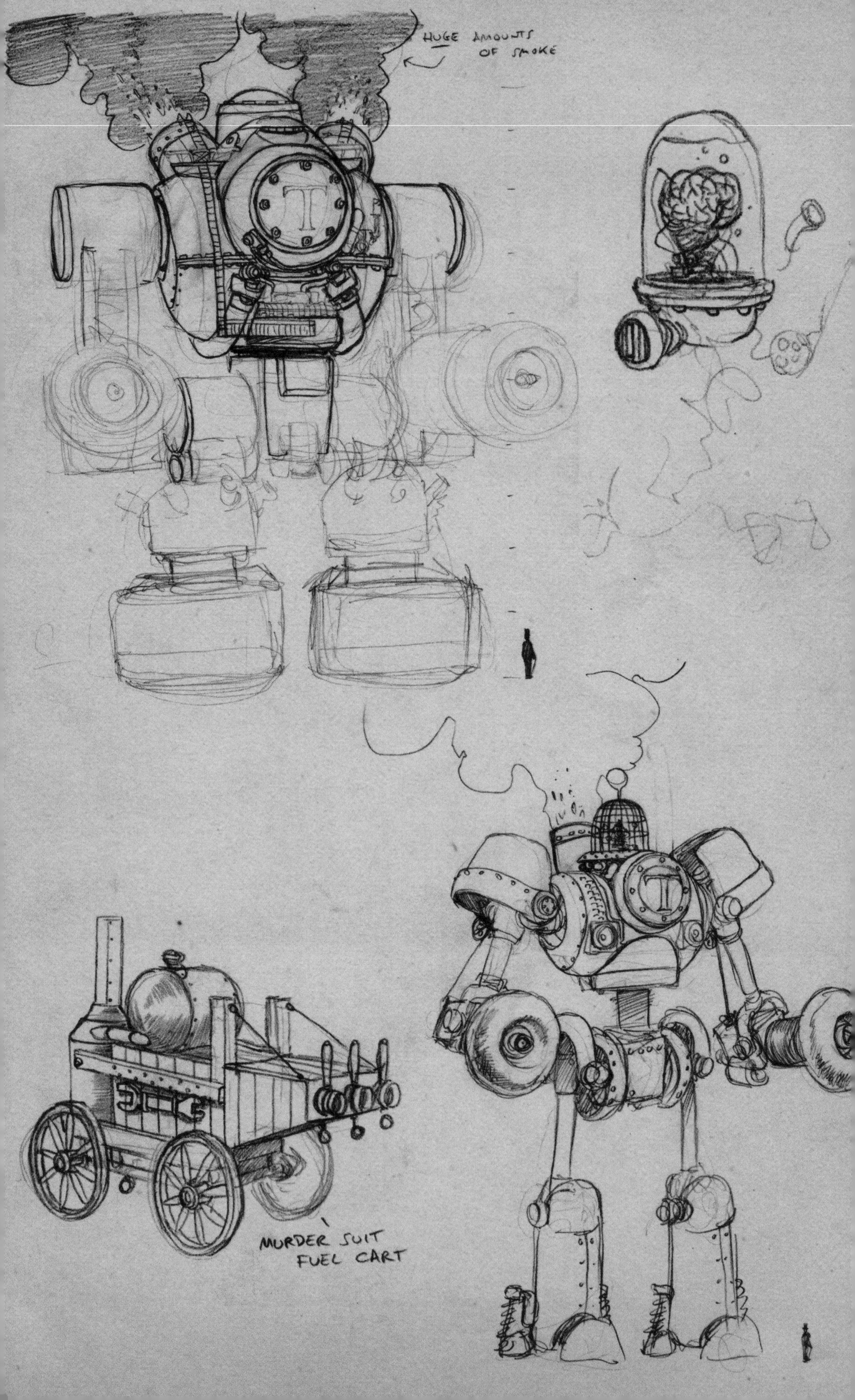
HUGE AMOUNTS OF SMOKE
MURDER SUIT FUEL CART

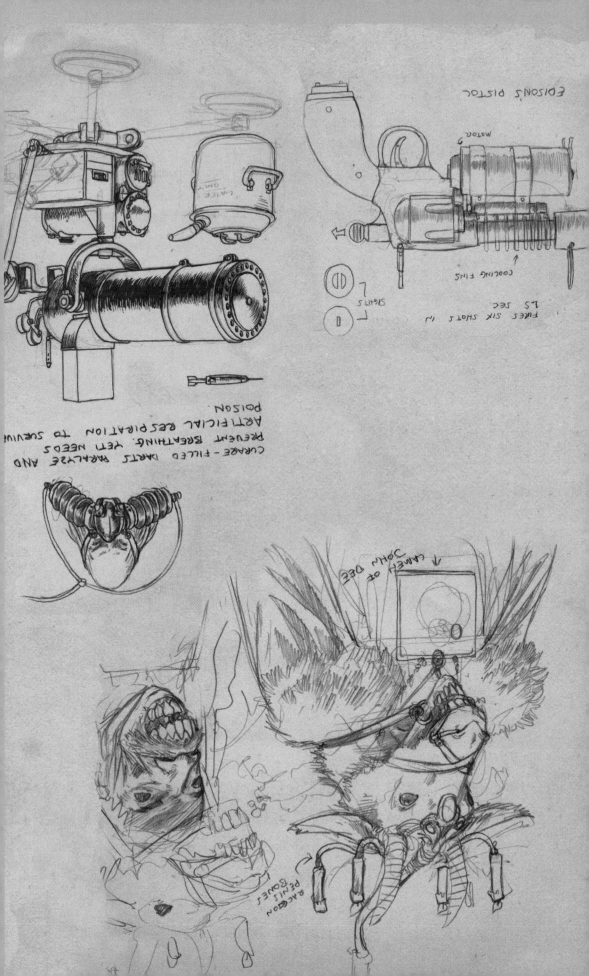

EDISON'S PISTOL

MOTOR

COOLING FINS

FIRES SIX SHOTS IN 1.5 SEC

SIGHTS

WATER ONLY

POISON

CURARE-FILLED DARTS PARALYZE AND
PREVENT BREATHING, YETI NEEDS
ARTIFICIAL RESPIRATION TO SURVIVE

CAMERA OF
JOHN DEE

RACCOON
PENIS
BONES

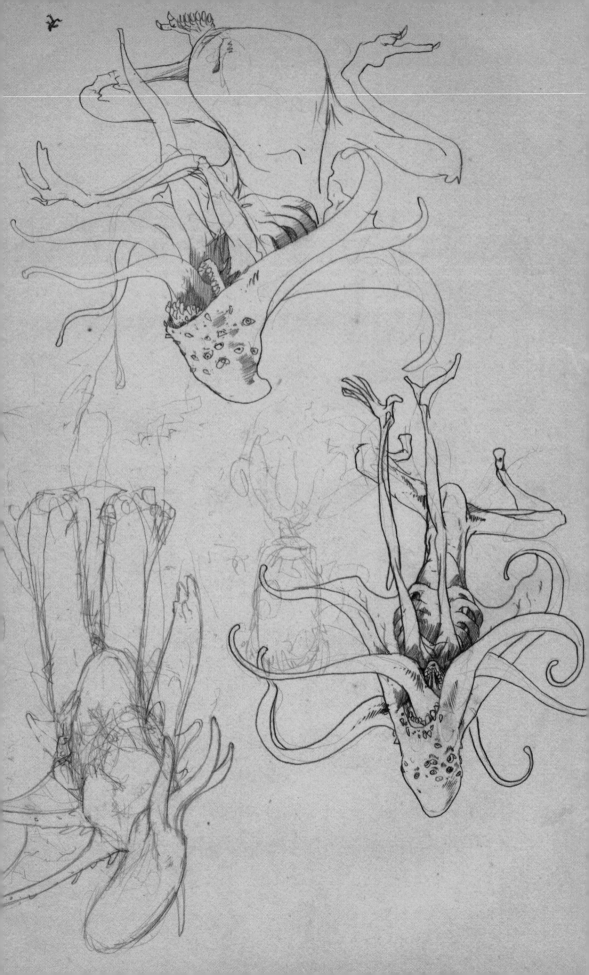